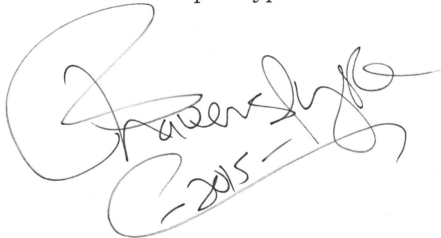

This is our new reality.

The Zombie Apocalypse is real.

THE MISADVENTURES OF TWO RELUCTANT

ZOMBIE HUNTERS

~ZOMBIES AT THE CON~

By

RHAVENSFYRE

THE MISADVENTURES OF TWO RELUCTANT ZOMBIE HUNTERS: Zombies at the Con

Acknowledgements

To our lovely Beta Readers: Gail, Tammy, Dava and Marion. Thank you for taking this trip with us while we explored the new, and somewhat disgusting world of the Zombie Apocalypse. Thank you for laughing along with the humor, and shuddering at the gross bits, proving that even if zombies aren't normally your thing, you can still enjoy a great read. We wove this tale for all of you, neophytes and hard core Zombie aficionados, both.

May 16, 2019 (Otherwise known as the day the world went to hell.)

It's a beautiful day for a zombie apocalypse.

I don't know why it couldn't be an overcast crappy day. No, it had to be a bright summer day. The type of day you just know is going to be perfect. That just goes to show you that even Mother Nature can be a sarcastic bitch with a unique sense of humor.

But, I guess I am getting ahead of myself. It's just been one of those days and it's not even over yet. We still have to make it back to our house, 60 miles away.

Let me introduce myself. My name is KL. Yes, those are just my initials, but after today I really don't know if full names are important anymore, they sure don't seem so when you're counting every breath. Proper names just seem wasteful. It's all about survival now, and that means conserving. Energy, food, gas, time...everything and anything that will ensure your survival...or at least get you better odds to see the next sunrise.

I, along with my wife, Roxy, belong to a zombie group. You know, one of those fun groups where you pretend to fight zombies. You go around with your friends and act all big and bad and use fake weapons to knock down people with moulage on their faces, pretending to be dead while they shamble around and moan louder than they probably ever do between the sheets. Actually, that should be past tense. They still amble and moan, but you find out real quick that a knee to the groin ain't going to do shit to stop a zombie.

That's where our story starts. I don't know why or how, and I have to say I really don't care, but the two of us ended up having front row center seats to a real life apocalypse. A zombie apocalypse. I feel like I'm stuck in a bad B movie, with no way out and no way to hit the fast forward button so I can cheat and find out how the movie ends. All I know for sure is...

It was all fun and games until shit got real.

KL

6 a.m.

"I can't believe they are so anal about weapons here. I can't even bring untipped arrows."

Roxy, my wife and cohort in all things good and evil, cast a glance over at me and raised her eyebrow. I knew what that look meant, but I ignored it like I always did. Yes, I was pouting, and yes, I felt I was justified in railing against the injustice of idiotic rules meant to keep people safe from themselves, much like those lovely padded walls they kept in a psych ward. Only I didn't need protecting from myself, and you can't pad every wall in the universe just in case someone develops a case of awkwardness and trips on a patch of gravity. I mean, really? What the hell do you do with a bow and no arrows? It just looks stupid, you know? But the costume required a bow, and I was committed to wearing the most badass and awesome costume at the con, so I was reduced to grumbling in the passenger seat while Roxy drove and pretended not to think it was all so very funny.

"It didn't stop you from bringing them though, did it?" Roxy asked. The corner of her mouth curled into an endearing half smile that spoke volumes. She really was my cohort in crime, and she knew me too well.

"Maybe," I muttered. There was no reason to give up all my secrets, eh? She was right nonetheless. Except I didn't bring the untipped ones used for show, like the ones the Cosplayer's used. Nope. I brought my actual arrows, the sharp pointy ones that worked for real. Why? Just because, that's why. It feels too weird to carry a bow around but not have my arrows. I know, I know...the rent-a-cops at the door won't let me bring them in, but at least I'll know they'll be comfortably close...outside in the Zombie Mobile.

"Yeah, well you brought your gun," I shot back, more amused than anything else.

"I did, but you don't see me moaning about having to leave it in the truck." Miss Reasonable smirked at me before turning her attention back on driving.

"Yeah, Yeah. Whatever." That little comment earned me a derisive snort. You see, Roxy is a lot like me. We are always prepared. No, not for zombies, that gig's just for fun...it's living, breathing people that are the real danger, well, just a few of them.

Before you get the wrong impression of either of us, we aren't a couple of those "gun nutters" like an English friend of ours calls us crazy Americans. It's just that with the way the country was going all to hell lately, neither one of us was willing to be caught unprepared. You would think that with all the nastiness going on in the world, things like comic book conventions and other nerdy venues would have given up and gone the way of the dodo, but they've actually been thriving.

Maybe it had to do with the need for escapism, or perhaps it had to do with a desperate need for some real life superheroes in this dirty, bloody universe we've made for ourselves. I haven't a clue. All I know is there is big money in the Con and dressing up and pretending to kill zombies is a big ticket item.

Besides, it's just too much fun pumping gas in the backwoods of North Carolina in a long black sleeveless fitted coat and black hat...all decked out in my leather bracers and sporting a nifty cross-back harness meant to carry steel and wood, not foam and plastic.

The fake polypropylene weapons insulted my general sense of badassery, but thanks to a little model paint and a bit of artistic license, they looked pretty real. Real enough that I had to have my fake weapons checked every time I left the floor during the last Con to use the bathroom. Good thing it was always on the way back, it might have gotten ugly if they had kept me from the facilities after sucking down soda all day.

We finally reached our freeway exit, and I straightened up out of my comfortable slouch so I could pay attention to where we were going. I actually took my job as co-pilot pretty seriously, but only for street traffic. Roxy, the truck, and freeway speeds were all things generally better left ignored, mostly for my mental health. She had this weird rule about the "law of gross tonnage", which generally meant if you were smaller than she was, you should get out of the way. According to her, it was the polite thing to do. I think she learned it from her time in the Army, back when she drove big ass trucks for a living. She told me what they were called, but I have to admit...I hear Army story and all of a sudden I'm in a Peanuts cartoon and the teacher is saying "wah-wah-wah."

Blame it on the ADD.

I do remember that it had eight wheels and eight wheel drive, which sounds like something I could really get into, but since the chances of that ever happening is next to nil, why get my hopes up? Now she was reduced to driving what we lovingly called the Zombie Mobile, our Toyota Tundra. We had decked it out with Zombie Response stickers, a light bar, and a cow catcher on the front. It was huge, but not huge enough for her...I could just tell by the gleam in her eye when something bigger and badder rumbled by, but it was enough for me. It also looked official enough that at times we would actually get stopped by people asking if we were for real. That was always good for a laugh. Sometimes we played along for fun, sometimes just to be a bit evil. I mean, really? They actually believed the Zombie Response Team was a real offshoot of the

CDC. We just warned them not to go to Wally World after midnight, just in case.

"Um, Roxy? The sky looks kind of weird today."

It was early, and we were close to the ocean, so it usually took a while for the sun to burn off the morning fog that often lingered along the coastline. Except today looked different. The heavy cloudbank in front of the sun wasn't its normal drab, gray, humidity generating mass of yuck. It glowed, not brilliantly, but in a greasy, southern fried sort of way that reminded me of something else. It took me a moment, but when the light shifted and took on a creepy greenish yellow 3D tinge, I made the connection. It looked like pictures I had seen of the Northern Lights, and that was something we just didn't get in North Carolina.

"Most people call that a sunrise, you know."

My wife, the smart ass.

"I am aware. Just because I am not normally up at this time does not mean I've never seen one before." Yeah, I can give it as well as I take it. That's why we work so well together. We speak the same language, sarcasm, only mine comes with a southern drawl. "But seriously, doesn't that cloud bank look kind of weird... No! Wait till we get to a stop light to look. Jeez. I really don't feel like having to call a tow truck to get out of a ditch this early."

Swerving at 65 miles an hour was about as exciting as touching a hot wire, the electrical kind you might find in say, one of those emergency defibrillator kits. The heart pounding in your throat sensation wasn't pleasant, either, so if I sounded a little freaked out or yelled a bit, it was too bad for her. I wasn't going to apologize.

"You said look. I looked," Roxy said, remarkably unruffled despite swerving halfway out of our lane just a few seconds ago. She squinted up at the sky for barely a half second, managing to keep the truck in a straight line this time. "Yeah that is unusual looking. Is there supposed to be rain today?"

"No, but it is North Carolina, so who knows? It's a nice day, otherwise." It was. Not too hot and not too cold, a regular fairy tale day it was. Yeah, right.

"Morning."

"What?"

"It's too early. It's still morning," Roxy enunciated the hated word slowly and loudly, then grinned at me. "As in, Good Morning."

"Fine, it's a good morning." I threw up my hands in exasperation. And people wonder why I am not a morning person.

The bitchy GPS voice chimed in, barking at us to turn right at the next light. The GPS and Roxy have a hate/hate relationship, which is why I'm in charge of directions. Lucky for me, the convention center was only a block off the freeway exit and it was too early on a Saturday morning for any sane person to be up and moving so we pretty much had the road all to ourselves. All I had to do was find the right parking lot so we could unload.

"Turn right here," I said, checking the email on my phone to verify which loading dock to go to. "We can unload in the back there."

A few people were already there. Most of them were busy unloading boxes and ducking into the convention center through a huge metal docking bay door, but there was an equal number of guys standing next to the dumpster choking down doughnuts and coffee like it was their last meal. When I jumped out of the truck, the sickly sweet smell mixed with coffee and exhaust fumes sent my system into a state of confusion. It's awful hard trying not to breathe Carbon Monoxide when it's mixed with the yummy combination of bread and caffeine tempting an empty stomach. You just want to inhale as deeply as possible and hope for a second-hand sugar high.

"Do you think they will actually check for real knives?" My hand wandered to the metal clip tucked into my waistband. My go to knife, otherwise known as "KL daily wear", was a nifty little Spyderco folder that Roxy had bought me last spring. It was legal in most states that allowed serrated edge folders, and I never left home without it.

"Probably. You might as well leave it in the truck. We don't need a repeat of the concert incident."

She was right. We had gone to an Aerosmith concert a couple of years ago and I forgot I had my regular pocket knife on me...not even a major thing. But I had to trek it all the way back to the truck to put it away or have it confiscated. I was lucky they saw me as a girl and not someone dangerous. Silly people. I did miss the first song for the opening act, and that pissed me off. Lesson learned.

We now refer to that as the concert incident.

"It's ridiculous. I should be allowed to protect myself," I grumbled, determined to be huffy about it. I am not big on crowds but this Con only came around once a year and the local zombie group wanted to have a showing there. Yeah, we belong to a zombie group. As raggedy of a little band of dystopian wannabee's as you'd ever lay eyes on, but they were fun...geeky in a paramilitary sort of way that only other zombie aficionado's truly understand.

"Well, you can always accidently smack someone with your bow if you have too," Roxy suggested, then clapped her hand over her eyes and shook her head when I looked a little too enthusiastic about the idea. "You know I was just joking, right?"

"Sure I do!" I exclaimed, then gave her a quick peck on the cheek before ducking away. I know she was trying to get me to laugh and relax but she also knows I like to have my options open. I have my own book of rules just like she does, and in my book, shins are always fair game.

"Uh, huh. Come on gorgeous, these boxes won't unload themselves." Roxy pulled out the dolly and loaded a few boxes herself before realizing I wasn't helping. I was busy watching the sky.

"Now what?"

"Are you sure the sky doesn't look weird to you?"

Roxy shrugged. "I don't know. Maybe they're offshore bombing this weekend?"

"Maybe." The rest of the boxes went on the dolly, but I couldn't honestly say how much of the work was mine versus hers. I just couldn't stop thinking about the odd sunrise.

"Hey, the rest of the guys are here." Roxy's voice broke into my thoughts. "Are you ready?"

"As I'll ever be."

"Great! Let's get this party started. Time to kill zombies and entertain the kiddies, hmm."

"Oh, my God, you did not just say that."

Roxy laughed and pulled me in through the bay doors, smack dab into the middle of all the noise and controlled chaos of the local Con. The metal door rattled on the way down, clanging loudly against the concrete floor before being locked up tight. Before they closed completely, I finally caught sight of the sun. Just now clearing the trees and riding a bright blue sky, it looked completely normal.

Roxy

Well, I have to say I was surprised, but we managed to make it through the first hour of con without a single incident. Well, sort of. KL managed to behave herself for the most part. So far, she's only smacked one person accidently-on-purpose with her bow. I would have almost believed it was truly an accident if the hit hadn't been so well aimed and if she hadn't looked back and smiled at me with that Cheshire cat grin of hers. I mean, what would you do if you walked into the bathroom only to find some half-dressed woman balancing on the edge of the sink while she shaves her armpits? I have to wash my hands there, not to mention, just eww. I have to give props to KL though. She managed to avert her eyes and get her business done while avoiding the woman. Unfortunately, the woman wasn't a customer, she was another exhibitor.

Underdressed in a multicolored little costume that fell somewhere between Strawberry Shortcake and Jeannie, with an excessive amount of pale skin between item A and B, she was way too bouncy for my poor wife. KL was crammed between two tables trying to eye an interesting little display of crystals

13

when candy cotton pink hair and knee high boots trapped her inside a one way maze.

It was the woman from the bathroom.

Then she started talking, or I should say babbling in that fake girly child voice that some women seem to think men like. Think Betty Boop on helium and happy pills, except that the boobs spilling outside the top of her bodice churned when she moved, as if some ancient sea creature was swimming just beneath the surface but never breached. At that point, I have to say she got off easy just getting rapped across the shins with a bow. KL made her escape, and we were off, diving back into the crowd to do our job.

Our job is to look interesting, walk through the crowd, and send people over to the booth where our local zombie group is. Every so often one of our zombies will jump out of the crowd and we have a fake tussle. It's fun and more importantly, it's not boring, not like sitting in the booth and doing the hard sell like the other girls. T-shirts, stickers, memberships to the zombie response team and the big ticket items you have to watch so they don't walk away. Mostly bug-out bags. Backpacks in camouflage with everything you need to survive the apocalypse in one handy package. Keep them in your car, under your bed...whatever your level of paranoia requires to feel safe. Band-Aids and water treatment pills, para-cord and those little metallic blankets that are supposed to keep you from getting hyperthermia, all for just over two hundred bucks.

Most of the other zombie hunters are guys, Jason, Tommy and Bobby. Jason—not his real name—is a scary sucker. Bald, tall and totally into his movie alter ego...yeah, that Jason is his hero. He's good for looming and he loves camo paint way too much. Tommy is an Army wannabe who hangs out at the local thrift/military surplus store, and Bobby doesn't talk—ever. He actually was in the military. He's skinny as a rail and he's never alone, in fact he's so far up Tommy's ass he might as well be his shadow. I have a feeling that if the shit ever hit the fan, he'd be the first one to hit the deck, then go all Rambo on us. I watch him closely, much in the same way I watch a dog I'm not sure will bite if anyone moves too fast around them. Then there's Brandon, Paul and Lauren. That's the core group, plus or minus a few that float in and out whenever they can. The zombies are all local volunteers that get free face paint for their troubles. It's all good.

"Are you bored already?" KL bumped into me just enough to get my attention.

"Hmm?" I asked, tearing my eyes away from a pretty little bauble I thought she might like.

"You're scowling."

"So? Maybe I'm practicing my Zombie Hunter face. We're supposed to be stalking zombies, right? I'm just in character." That was a better excuse than what I was really doing. It's hard staying out of shopping mode with all the excited noise surrounding me. A Con is sort of like a carnival, replete with greasy food, bad music, costumed players and lots and lots of stuff I don't need for sale. I love carnivals.

"You're shopping, not hunting," KL smirked, then pointed across the hall. "There they are, just in case you haven't noticed."

She had spotted a small band of Zombies sneaking around by the food court. It kind of ruins the effect when they're being crafty. Zombies aren't known for their stealthy moves. I shook my head. "Jeez, they're trying too hard."

"Ooh, can we get a picture with you?" an overly excited middle aged woman in flip flops and a Doctor Who t-shirt stopped us in the middle of the aisle. She wrapped her arm around KL's bare bicep and turned towards someone I supposed was her husband. I had to smile. She got that a lot. She did look pretty badass, and that black cowboy hat was like a siren song to some of the ladies, a few of the guys, and a couple of unidentified Furries in horse costume.

"Sure." KL stepped into the center of the aisle and pulled out her short sword. Tall and thin and all tatted up, she looked like she just stepped out of a *Revenant Chaser* comic book. Since she was the model for RC, it was so very convenient she liked to dress up for me. It made sketching up the scenes for the next edition that much easier.

There was no way I was going to outshine her—no matter what I wore, so I had gone with comfortable. I was perfectly happy in my discrete khaki pants, old combat boots, and vest. It was KL's job to protect me, and my job to film everything. I guess that made me the sidekick.

"Babe?" KL looked at me. I nodded and lifted my camera.

With her long bow across her back and leather bracers on both forearms, she dropped her head just enough to put her face in shadow. It was perfect. Instantly formidable and dark and I swear the woman almost squealed in delight. The hubby snapped a quick shot off with his phone, I got my shots in, and just before they ran off I remembered to hand them a pamphlet. "Hey, don't forget to run by our booth for all your zombie hunting needs!"

KL sheathed her sword before shaking her head. Clearly amused, she took off her black Stetson for a second, exposing a wild shock of blonde hair that she promptly scrubbed into an even wilder mess. "Wow."

"They like seeing the character." Ever defending the masses, never mind the fact she gets more attention than the one penning all the artwork.

"Yeah. You missed the twin goths asking me why I was fighting zombies when I'm supposed to be hunting down rogue vampires."

"What did you tell them?"

"That I was bored, so I thought I'd expand my repertoire." KL put her hat back on then lightly flicked her fingertips against the rim to get it positioned just so, off kilter just enough to make her look roguish. We started walking again.

"Huh, that's weird." KL stopped dead in her tracks.

"What?" I grumbled, rubbing my elbow. Bouncing into her hurt.

"It just got very quiet," KL spoke in a hushed tone. "The noise just stopped. Have you ever been to a convention and heard nothing, just complete and utter silence?"

"No, I haven't." I felt the small hairs on the back of my neck rise. It wasn't really completely noiseless, not with the background music still blaring through the convention speakers. But that roaring white noise a large crowd made, like water crashing onto boulders beneath a waterfall? THAT had gone from deafening to nothing—zero decibels— as if someone had muted every single human voice in the building but only after exhaling one last collective sigh. My skin started to crawl. "I don't like this. I think we should head back to the booth and see what is going on."

We moved out, weaving in and out of the crowd as easily as the shuttle slipped through the handloom. Everyone was moving so slow. Between the silence and slow as molasses movement of the crowd around us, the sensation of disconnect between us and reality made my head spin. I took KL's hand and squeezed it. There was no way I was letting that hand go until we got where we were going.

"Do you feel it?" she asked.

"Yeah. I guess this is what a bad acid trip feels like." I shook my head, trying to clear the cotton ball stuffed in my ears sensation. Something was not right. Actually, something was very, very, wrong. We weren't just wading through human molasses spills, we were dodging mannequins. Not a single person other than ourselves was moving. That's probably why I almost jumped 10 feet when another voice broke through the silence and called out for us, an impressive feat when you're barely 5 feet tall to start with.

"Roxy, KL, what's going on?" Lauren, one of our Zombie team members emerged from behind a frozen Batman. If I was short, Lauren was what you would call Pixie size. The only reason she stood eye to eye with me was her shoes. She had found combat boots somewhere with 4 inch heels and she still managed to walk around like a dystopian badass, all the way down to duel drop-leg thigh holsters and lace trimmed fingerless gloves. She had a style of her own, that one, but right now she just looked worried.

KL and I glanced at each other.

"We were about to ask you the same thing." It was cute that Lauren thought we had any answers, but I was too happy to see another breathing, talking and walking person to care.

"Is this some sort of flash mob thing?" she asked, eyeing the unmoving crowd surrounding us. Her right hand flexed and I could tell she was wishing there was something more than plastic cap guns resting just beneath her fingertips. I knew because I was feeling pretty much the same way.

"You think? I've seen something like this before on the internet, but never with so many people." That would be an impressive feat. I craned my neck around, looking for hidden cameras and not finding them or my wishful thinking anywhere in the building.

"And what? We are the only ones not in the know, out of thousands of people...really?" KL drawled. Not once did her eyes leave the crowd around her.

I almost laughed out loud, almost...but the urge to remain quiet was, ironically, screaming a warning inside my head loud and clear. "Leave it to you to find a place for sarcasm in the middle of an unknown event."

"Sarcasm is an art that, once learned, can never be unlearned." KL managed to intone that malarkey with a straight face. I stared at her for a full 20 seconds before her lip twitched and she winked at me.

"This is just too freaky," I said to my wife and Lauren. "I think we should head to the booth. At least it's in the corner away from the main part of the floor. Lauren, can you try calling the guys and seeing where they are?" I reminded her that she had one of the walkie-talkies. So did a few of the guys.

"Um, no need. I see them right now," KL said, pointing with her bow towards the upstairs balcony. "Looks like Brandon and Paul."

The Walkie squelched. Everyone jumped and I gave Lauren a dirty look. She fumbled with the Walkie and almost dropped it before dialing down the volume, then started talking. "Copy that." Lauren nodded and gave us a thumbs up, then gestured towards the booth. "They said they'll meet us there."

"I hope," KL muttered. She didn't sound very confident, and for a moment there I wasn't sure if she was doubting our ability or the guys, but she started moving her legs and that was all I needed right now. Cooperation.

Getting back to the booth was a weird game of slide, slide, sidle, sidle, tramp forward and then backtrack to avoid the randomly placed bodies standing there like leftovers from a wax museum exhibit. I waved my hand in front of a polite looking man all decked out in an awesome steampunk costume, then snapped my fingers just to see what would happen. No flinch, nothing...just a 1,000 yard stare that looked through and past me. Our very own frozen tin man decked out in bronze and copper and sporting a 19th century top hat. He didn't carry

21

an ax, but his walking cane looked mildly dangerous so I grabbed onto it and tugged and he almost toppled over onto me. I almost screamed, and I did step back, then stood there listening to my heart pound in my chest and wishing I didn't have so much caffeine on board. Believe me when I say adrenaline was doing a fine job keeping me wide awake right now. I ended up forcefully uncurling each finger to liberate the walking cane, then danced away in a sadly geeky little victory dance that ended in a KL salute. One finger in the air, I waved that in the man's face. "Ha! Screw you, you creepy bastard."

Then I took a closer look at my prize. "Oh, score! Looky here at what I found."

A quick twist of the wrist separated the cane about 8 inches down from the crown. The hiss of metal against metal revealed a very illegal and very nice bit of steel.

"A sword cane?" Lauren asked. "How the heck did he slip that in?"
From the tone of her voice, you could tell she was impressed. So was I. KL just frowned, no doubt regretting that her much loved Spyderco was tucked away in the Zombie Mobile.

"No idea. But it's mine now until we figure out what's going on." I slid the blade home but didn't twist the handle tight. No need to make things harder than they had to be.

"Do you see any of them breathing? Or blinking? Anything?" Lauren hugged herself while she walked, those damn stiletto heels clacking against the linoleum with every step. If there was anyone else moving around in here, she was as good as an echo locator broadcasting our location. I wasn't sure that was a good idea.

"Uh, Lauren? Maybe those boots should come off for now?"

The string of curses that followed my suggestion were as colorful as any Sailor's and just as creative, but she took them off.

"Thanks, Roxy. I owe you one." Lauren stared up at me with eyes as big as saucers, all 4 feet 9 inches of her.

"No problem," I said, lying through my teeth. What I really wanted to say was, yeah, you do. We had both seen enough horror movies to know the cute little girl in heels was the first to die. She could never outrun the killer, and she never had the foresight to take off her shoes before he caught her.

Unfortunately, now she was lighter and faster than we were. The old joke about not having to run fast, you just had to be able to run faster than somebody else came to mind. Now I'd have to resort to tripping if it came right down to it. My chivalric streak was pretty wide, but not so wide I would sacrifice myself or KL for someone else in the event of zombies, vampires, an alien invasion, or any other cataclysmic event that resulted in total chaos.

23

Don't judge me. I never said I was perfect, just practical.

"Hey, guys. Check this out."

I turned to find KL poking people with her bow and freaked out instantly. "What the hell are you doing?" I hissed, taking a wild swipe at KL's bow but missing.

"There's no response...look." She pokes one, then another, all with same outcome—nothing. Then she gets to the fourth one.

"Hey look, isn't this the lady from this morning?" KL asks, tipping her head to the side and squinting at the woman. "The cotton candy hair lady from the bathroom, Miss Shaves-in-Public?"

"Yeah, I think so, but now she looks more like an oversized Raggedy Ann doll."

"Dolls don't stand up on their own." KL narrowed her eyes and leaned in closer, until she was almost nose to nose with the woman. Then she poked her with the sharp end of her bow again. What happened next would have been funny if I wasn't already freaked the hell out. Miss SIP squeaked, KL jumped back and we all screamed, just a little bit.

"What the hell?" I yelled. Lauren clamped her hand over her mouth and whimpered. She got a withering look from KL for that, who promptly went back to poke the bear, so to speak, one more time.

"I don't think that's a good idea," I warned her, but it was no use. She does the same thing with snakes. I stopped asking her not to a long time ago, it just encourages her to misbehave. I know KL heard me because her lip curled.

"Please don't."

"Crap, KL, you just had to poke the bear didn't you?" I stepped back, falling into a fighting stance and pulling out my pilfered blade. Was that an overreaction on my part? Not after this morning, and certainly not after the entire Con turned into Mannequin city.

A pair of very scared, very wide eyes gleamed under the harsh fluorescent lights. Her gaze shifted towards each of us in turn, but she stood stock still, as if she was afraid to move. It was a dead giveaway, literally, that she wasn't like the others around her. I smirked. Even creepy weirdness couldn't stop the puns from coming.

KL was prone to a more direct method. She grabbed the woman by the sleeve of her dress and pulled her closer, away from the nest of still bodies she had been hiding in.

"What are you doing, just standing there?" Gruff, demanding, and oozing leather studded menace, my wife managed to frighten away what little hint of color the woman possessed. The blood drained from her face until she was as white as the concrete walls surrounding us, and I prayed that she wasn't as dense.

"Well I didn't know what was going on or who you were, so I thought silence was next best course."

"That actually makes sense." KL looked to me, waiting for my consensus. I stared at the woman for a moment, then shrugged.

"The more the merrier, I guess." I didn't see much in her if we needed her in a fight, but she was a warm body—a warm moving body—and that seemed to be something in short supply right now. "But I have two rules if you're going to hang with us."

"Anything."

"One. You need to talk like a grown up, not like some pre-pubescent chew toy for creepy boys." I held up two fingers. "Two. Please tell me that is a wig."

"It is," she replied eagerly.

"Good. Take it off." I whirled around without waiting for a yes. There were already more important things rolling through my mind and all the questions without answers were starting to put me in a bad mood. "Let's get going, people. I need to know if this...whatever this is...is limited to the Con or going on outside too."

From the look on their faces, that question hadn't occurred to them yet. For all we knew, there were a million people out there waiting for moss to start growing on their shoes and I needed to know that.

Behind me I could hear them talking.

"Come on, you can come with us to the booth. We're just waiting for our group to show up." That was Lauren, always so eager to help out. It actually made me happy. She could mother hen with the best of them, and that meant I didn't have to. "What's your name?"

"Anna, Ann," she answered. I swear my brain spasmed from the nails on chalkboard sound of the woman's voice.

"Well which is it, Anna or Ann?" I heard my wife inquire.

I whirled on them. She got a finger in the chest and KL got glared at. "I told you, no more little girl voice. You're what? Twenty-five? Not five or even fifteen. Sucking your thumb won't get you shit right now. And you? STOP POKING EVERYONE." I didn't yell, but it was close.

"Is she always this scary?"

"Oh, she's not scary, just mean," KL replied, sounding way too cheery. "I'm the scary one."

I grinned. Leave it to KL to find a way to keep someone from being chatty with her.

"Would you stop being so grumpy? You already poked her with your bow, stop trying to scare her," Lauren admonished her despite sounding just as grumpy as the rest of us.

"Alright already, I'll try to behave. This is just freaking the shit out of me and I have to pee. But I won't apologize for poking Anna—Ann, since I didn't know she was awake."

For KL that was actually nice. Don't get me wrong. She's a wonderful wife and very loving to her family...it's just the rest of society.

"It's okay...but, um I have to pee," Ann shyly admitted.

"Oh, good God, really?" I threw up my hands, then took a deep breath and tried to ignore the throbbing starting up behind my left eye. So close to our destination and yet so far. I sighed and turned around to face my little band of misfits. "And you, Lauren?"

"Yeah, I could go."

This time I did break down and rub my temples. This was getting painful.

"Alright, I guess we should all head to the restroom. We shouldn't separate, that's for sure."

I wanted to laugh at the irony. Women have been going to the bathroom in pairs for years and I have to say this is the first time I could remember where there was truly a good reason for the practice and it had nothing to do with gossip or girl talk. It was closer to some weird Pavlovian conditioning that made your bladder wake up the minute someone mentioned needing to pee or, worse yet, the second you walked into a restroom even if you had no intention of going.

Great, now I have to pee.

KL

I've never understood group bathroom breaks as a steadfast cultural pastime for women and despite all the weirdness, today was no exception.

Roxy went in first since she was the only one armed with anything that could do some harm. My plastic sword was good for show and maybe smacking someone in the ass if they thought that was fun, but as a weapon? I guess if I pummeled someone about the head with it they might develop a nasty headache and a bad attitude, but I doubt if I could accomplish any real damage.

The bathroom was as silent as a tomb inside its cheap tiled walls. Roxy scowled and pulled her sword blade loose before heading down the thin isle of stalls. A palm to each stall door resulted in a loud rattle but they stayed stubbornly closed. I tried not to think about it, but I couldn't keep the images of mannequin like women sitting on their porcelain thrones with their pants wrapped around their knees. All I can say is that whatever was happening to these people, it must have stopped all bodily functions. No one was peeing, and at least one stall needed a courtesy flush. From the look on Ann's face, I wasn't the only one not enjoying that aroma.

My nerves were rapidly fraying into a tight bundle of exposed wires that poked at my inner calm, mostly because of Ann. Our newest member was a veritable fount of questions that I had no answers to. She reminded me of an overly curious child who loved to hear "I don't know." After the fourth question, I turned on her and growled. "I don't know why nobody is moving, I don't know why we are moving, I don't know if or when they will start moving and I certainly don't know what the hell is going on anywhere else." I thought that would shut her up, but it didn't. My outburst only encouraged her.

"Shouldn't there be something about this in the news or on the internet?" she asked.

"What did you say?" I spun around so swiftly my coat tails flew up and made a swooshing noise as the heavy black canvas cloth cut through the air. "Never mind. Jesus..." I grumbled, then started digging around for my phone. After the first pat down, I remembered that I had left the damn thing in the truck.

"Roxy? Do you have your phone?" Some people might have been embarrassed asking that question, but not me. I'm not married to my phone like some people are, so sue me.

"Yeah. I do." She pulled out her phone and hit a few buttons. The longer she spent staring at the screen the deeper she scowled and the antsier I got.

She looked up at me, and from the look on her face, it wasn't good news. "I got nothing."

"No news?" I asked. That was a surprise. Everything ended up on the internet and with social media the way it was, it was often out there in real time. Maybe not accurately, but people were always talking about everything and anything.

"That's not what I said. I said I got nothing. No bars, no service, nothing." She held up the phone so it faced us. "It's dead, and before you ask...yes, I checked to make sure it has a charge."

"So, we have no idea what's going on."

"Nope, I'm afraid not."

"This bites. Do you think this is happening everywhere?" I asked, tossing my head in the general direction of our non-moving companions. Ann scowled at me, then smirked when Roxy used my own answer against me.

"I don't know."

It might have been coincidence that Roxy found an open stall at that same moment, but my question must have distracted her. She hit the door hard enough for me to hear her palm slap across the flat surface, it slammed open with a shotgun bang and everyone jumped. My gaze flew to the nearest non-moving person, a young woman in a powder blue princess costume that didn't look like something I would want to deal with in a public restroom...or ever. She didn't react to the sudden noise, but I couldn't stop staring, waiting for a blink that never came. The skin on the back of my neck crawled in that way it does when you know something is watching you and I turned slowly, half expecting to find a half dozen sets of unblinking eyes watching me.

"Okay, this is getting creepy, can we just do what we came here to do and get out of here?" Lauren asked. She had a point although I think getting creepy was a huge understatement. It was already beyond creepy, in a "calm before the storm" sort of way. I just couldn't dwell on it, just like I couldn't answer Ann's questions. All I could do was wait and see what was going to happen next and be ready for it. Playing junior detective just to find out what was going on sort of went on the back burner when you had to pee. I wasn't going to piss myself if one of these bastards started moving because I still had a full bladder.

I guess you could call that Rule Number 1 of zombie hunting: Always go into any unknown situation with an empty bladder. It's less embarrassing and you can run faster.

"I agree." Then, because I could...I called dibs on the toilet. Roxy went next.

"Here, it's the only weapon we have." Roxy handed me the cane sword on my way out. I grinned.

"Oh, yeah," I said, and gleefully started to unclip my costume sword.

"Hey, not so fast. I'm taking it back when I'm done," Roxy said. She must have been peeking at me through the crack in the door.

I retreated back towards the entrance. My badass self tried to make an excuse for me by saying I was taking point and protecting the others, but honestly, it had more to do with the silence. Imagine a women's bathroom with no noise. Peeing suddenly becomes very loud without background chatter. I chose to concentrate on something else before the smart ass in me reared her head and started having some fun playing the 'who has a shy bladder?' game. The non-moving folk on the other hand, they were fair game.

There was a gaggle of women lined up at the sink who had been applying their makeup when they just stopped, awkwardly leaning against the counter and staring at their reflection, their faces contorted into various shapes depending on what they were doing. One woman's arm was raised, applying mascara to her left eye. Another one was frozen in a bad parody of a Marilyn Monroe pose, her lips pursed as she pouted into the mirror. I was tempted to play around with their makeup and switch out the bright lipstick she clutched in her hand for another's eyeliner. Resisting temptation is not my strong suite.

The sound of a toilet flushing was an impetus to hurry. In a few seconds, Roxy would be out of the stall and ready to ruin any fun I wanted to have. I peeked out at the other two. Lauren and Ann weren't paying attention to me so I went for it. Stiff fingers fought my efforts to liberate the lipstick until I concentrated on uncurling one finger at a time. They really were mannequin like, which probably explained why they were all standing upright. If they were dead, they'd be limp piles of humans scattered about the floor. I couldn't keep myself from chuckling nervously. It could be worse, they could be trying to eat my face off. If this was a horror movie, there would have been a lot more screaming and fake blood squirting all over the screen by now.

"Shut up, KL," I whispered. There was no need to borrow trouble when we had enough as it was. Being a brat was more my speed, and that meant finishing up what I started. Lipstick in hand, I chose my second victim. She was tiny like Lauren, but in that bony anorexic way that made you want to throw a hamburger or two at her. Her fingers gave way with a lot less effort on my part, then easily reformed around the cylinder with a quick squeeze. I winced. She really felt too easy to break.

"Everybody ready?" Roxy's voice echoed through the bathroom. Serious but with that business as usual robustness I often found annoying, it seemed to do the trick with Lauren and Ann. They fell in behind her like good little recruits. Mouths shut and eyes wide open, they headed back out to the main floor with me in the lead and Roxy taking up the rear.

A couple of things had changed in the small amount of time we were gone. There were a few people wandering around now. They looked as perplexed as I felt and spoke in hushed tones that made the building sound like it was whispering bad dreams.

"Don't talk or make eye contact. They will just ask questions and we don't know what's going on any more than they do," I instruct Ann and Lauren. No one likes to get bad news, and if you're the ones that look organized then the next illogical jump usually involves anger, fear and the need to find a convenient target. I didn't want our group to be that convenient group. It was better to let everyone remain confused individuals, not a crazed mob looking for answers they weren't going to get.

"Are you sure? Maybe one of them knows something?"

This time it was Lauren.

"Really? Do they look like they know what's going on? They look like they just woke up from one bad dream only to find themselves in another. They don't know crap and I don't need more tagalongs. I just want to meet up with the guys at the booth and then get the hell out of here," I snarled, pointing at a small group of people weaving past a larger than life Ironman. They looked over at us and stuttered to a stop, fear and hope flowed across their faces in equal measure until I glowered at them and pulled the sword blade free a few inches. The steel flashed and sent them scurrying in the other direction. A soft touch on my hand calmed me and sent the blade back into its sheath.

"Gently, sweetheart. We still don't know what's happening," Roxy spoke in an even voice, but the look in her eyes told me what she was really thinking. She was measuring each and every other moving soul in that room and labeling them. Friend, foe, or cannon fodder, she had a good eye for assessing people. It was an old joke, a game between us when we were out in public...to label the people around us based on how aware they were of their surroundings. It was sort of like watching National Geographic and picking out the slow antelope. You know, the one that inevitably ended up being dinner for the lions crouched in the tall grass around them. I know I'm not the only one who does this. They're the same people that drive so damn slow behind the herd of cars on a busy road that you can't make a left turn because the next group behind them is already lapping them.

"Okay, I'm sorry I asked."

"Look, Lauren. The guys know what they're doing. We know what we're doing. I don't know any of these people or what they are capable of. It's better this way." I was serious, too. There could be hero's walking around out there, but there were cowards, too. You wouldn't know until it mattered, and then if you chose wrong, it was usually your ass that paid for it, not them. I wasn't being cruel, I just knew myself. I wasn't a hero...and it wasn't my job to save the world, just the one's I cared for, and that list was mighty small.

That would be Rule Number 2: Know your limitations and don't pretend to be someone you aren't.

"Hey, guys?"

Roxy had stopped walking. Something near the food court had gotten her attention enough to distract her from our goal.

"That's different," she said, pointing at a dark blue lump tucked behind the condiment bar.

"You wanna check it out?"

Roxy chewed on her lip for a second before making a decision. She nodded her head, then glanced down at the sword cane in my hand. "Yeah."

That dark lump had arms and legs and wore a uniform.

"Shit! Is that a cop?" Lauren asked.

"Don't know. Let's find out," I said. Poking the man didn't do anything, so I toed him a little harder.

"Oh, ick."

The man wasn't a cop, and he wasn't going to get up anytime soon, either. Half of his face was purple and black where all of his blood had pooled under the skin. He was the first truly dead person we'd seen and there was no guessing what the cause of death was. A huge chunk of hotdog fell out of his mouth when we rolled him, joining the crushed mess of meat, bread and mustard smeared across the front of his otherwise pristine shirt. I hunkered down next to him to get a closer look. "Hmm. Looks like he bit off more than he could chew."

"That's not funny!"

"If you say so," I said, poking the man one more time with the sword cane. It was actually a relief to see someone dead...and not moving. A lot of the uglier thoughts in the back of my head were allowed to relax. He was dead and not moving. The mannequin people around me were somehow not dead, and not moving. So far, the math was working in my favor and that made me very, very happy. I grinned up at the people staring at me like I had lost my marbles, then tapped his shoulder badge. "Rent a cop, not a real one."

For some reason that made everyone else happy, but I was a little disappointed. A real cop would have been armed, all this guy had on him was a gut and a nightstick. I couldn't even use his belt because, unlike the movies, death was an ugly messy event that usually included shitting and pissing yourself. He must have read the playbook because he had checked both those activities off his list.

I reached down, really wanting to close my eyes but not able to if I wanted to avoid any of the mess, and gingerly moved one cold, limp arm away from his belt. Ick was right. I hated this. Roxy was the one who dealt with dead things, not me.

"What are you doing?" my wife asked, finally noticing that I was still down here.

"Just borrowing a couple things." That was all I managed to choke out while holding my breath.

"Why?" I swear she sighed at me when she asked that.

"He doesn't need them now, and I always wanted a nightstick." It made sense to me.

"Well hurry up. I want to get back to the booth and then get the hell out of here."

"Right there with ya, babe. Here, you want my big stick?" I made a lewd gesture with the long end of the stick.

She just shook her head and chuckled. "Are you going to give me back the sharp pointy? Don't think I didn't notice you adopting it."

I clung to the sword cane as if she was going to actually pull it out of my hand, bringing it close to my chest and out of her reach. "No way! Here, take the nightstick. I can always steal another one." I looked around us, scanning for more bodies. "There's bound to be more rent a cops around."

"Fine, you keep looking while we're moving, but don't get too distracted." Roxy tried to give me a stern look, but she couldn't hold it. She stepped closer and lowered her voice. "If you see someone armed, any REAL cops, let me know. I'd rather collect any loose firearms in here before someone else gets the same idea."

"Good idea." We had seen real cops roaming around, enjoying the comfy gig that paid them overtime to deal with mostly harmless teens enjoying a moment of roll playing. That didn't stop them from coming in with pepper spray, Tasers, and 9mm sidearms. We had fallen behind a bit and realized we had lost Lauren and Ann. A happy squeal made us both wince, but we were too happy to see the familiar outline of the Zombie Response Team banner flying over our booth.

"Finally." I blew out my breath, relieved that we had made it to our first goal.

Paul and Brandon were there, waiting for us. Lauren had run the last few feet and was wrapped so tightly around Paul he couldn't breathe.

"What took you ladies so long?" Brandon asked.

"Bathroom break," Roxy piped up.

"Seriously, right now?"

"When ya gotta go, ya gotta go," I informed Brandon. Just because guys can pee anywhere, doesn't mean they can tease us for wanting a little privacy.

"Brandon, Paul, this is Ann. We don't know her but she is still among the moving so we brought her with us." I introduced her to the guys.

They nodded at her, then went back to talking tactics. We were all paranoid about new people in general and this totally off the wall situation was not helping our paranoia at all. Speaking of that.

"Hey, guys? Where's Jason?" We were missing a couple of people.

"He got tired of waiting and decided to do some recon towards the front entrance."

"Did you see anyone moving around up where you were?" Roxy asked the guys.

"A few here and there. Some were just meandering around, kinda stunned. Some were heading for the front, trying to leave," Paul answered.

"And some were scooping up comic books and running," Brandon added with a frown. You could tell he was disgusted by the behavior. "We didn't try to stop them."

"That was probably smart," Roxy said. "Getting out of here as soon as possible sounds good, too. Does anyone have any real weapons?"

A chorus of no's answered her. Roxy looked positively crestfallen, then took a deep breath before taking charge again.

"Look, I know you all don't like it, but if you see anything that you could defend yourself with, we need to grab it. It's not like we're going to be stealing comic books and collectibles." She shot a hard look over at Brandon, who looked like he was going to rebel. He had very specific feelings about thievery and theft in general. "It's not stealing, Brandon. This..." she waved her arm at the general madness surrounding them. "This is not normal, and normal rules can't apply, got it?"

He still didn't look convinced so I stepped in to help.

"I stole a nightstick," I announced. I even managed to sound proud about it while staring Brandon down. He wouldn't dare tell me I was wrong because he knew I was the same way. Like Roxy said, this was special circumstances.

"Oh cool, where is it?" Paul asked.

Brandon looked away and nodded, surrendering his high road attitude to practicality. I smirked. This is why Paul and I get along so well. He gets it.

"Roxy has it now, I'm going to get another one, though. If I get a chance."

"On the way out the door, babe. I think we should get out of here." Roxy does tend to stick to the point better than me. Without her, I might have gotten distracted. I really did want my own nightstick.

Roxy

The way Brandon hesitated to gaze wistfully at the Zombie Response Team booth made me thankful I hadn't received the next edition of Revenant Chaser. I would have had to leave every copy behind, and it was my ART. If I was willing to do that, you know there was no way I was going to pack up all the t-shirts, fake ID badges and bumper stickers neatly laid out on the display tables. There wasn't going to be any sales today, and no one seemed interested in stealing t-shirts.

A quick scan for anything loose and useful changed my mind. The overpriced bug out bags were something that could actually be beneficial, and thanks to a crappy economy and cheap customers, there were enough to go around. With more glee than it probably warranted, I snatched those bad boys up and started passing them out. "Here, take one. You might need it." I tossed one to Lauren, she nodded and hugged the heavy bag to her chest.

"What about everything else?" Brandon asked.

"I'm not hanging around long enough to take down all this crap, but if you want to, go right ahead." If sarcasm was a liquid, it would have been dripping down the walls right now. It was a stupid question so if I offended anyone, that was just too bad.

I liked Brandon, but sometimes he had a problem with testosterone...as in, I have it so I should be the one in charge. Screw that. I held out the last bag, dangling it in front of him by my fingertips. He had about 2.5 seconds to take it before I dropped it on the floor. "You want this, or are you going to quibble about it not being yours to take since you agreed to sell them for Mikey?"

Mikey wasn't here, and I highly doubted he was going to show up. If he wanted to settle up with me later, he could find me at home because that's where I was heading as soon as I could boogie out of here.

Brandon finally gave in and took the three steps necessary to grab the bag out of my hands, but he still managed to look like someone was making him do something he didn't want to.

I tried really hard not to grin at his butt-hurt expression and slipped the last pack over my own shoulders then adjusted the straps so they were comfortable and didn't restrict my movement. A quick roll of my shoulders and a practice spin of KL's pilfered nightstick and I was ready. "So are we ready to get going?"

"No."

We all turned to find Bobby standing not more than four feet away from us.

"Jesus Christ, Bobby. Don't sneak up on us like that," KL hissed. She beat me by half a second, and only because it took me a moment to remove my heart from my throat after damn near jumping out of my boots. Everyone else pretty much had the same expression on their face. They hadn't noticed him until that moment either. Until he spoke up, he had stood so quietly he had blended in with the mannequin folk. Hell, he still barely registered as more alive than they did, until you looked in his eyes.

"Sorry." Only the one word, muttered under his breath and accompanied by an unapologetic shrug. "Tommy is missing."

That was more words out of the man than he'd managed all morning.

"Aren't you always with Tommy? How could he be missing and you aren't?" I asked.

"We got separated in the crowd, now I can't find him."

"We should go look for him," Brandon said.

Of course.

KL grimaced and narrowed her eyes at Brandon. I could feel the displeasure radiating off of her in stiff, hot waves. She wasn't happy about that suggestion, and neither was I.

As we were all following Bobby back into the main part of the building KL pulled me aside. "I don't want to go back in there for that little piss-ant. He is probably hiding."

"I agree but it's best if we all stay together right now."

Tommy was an ELS, an entry level separation. He and Bobby had joined the Army at the same time on the buddy program but Tommy couldn't cut it. The funny thing was, he was still stuck in a holding company for weeks after Bobby graduated boot camp, all because he couldn't suck it up and drive on past a little homesickness. If you're not familiar with holding companies in the Army, I can tell you that it is pure hell for no particular purpose. At least boot camp ends in graduation and a career, but when the Army decides you aren't compatible with military life that doesn't mean they just let you go, nope. They make you do the most menial, nasty and boring crap they can think of. Believe me when I say the Army is an expert when it comes to excessive creativity in that department.

I'm not usually such a hardass, but I know him. He's the type that tries to do the minimum amount of work and then takes all the credit. That attitude didn't fly in the Army, and out he went. He still likes to tell strangers that he was in the Army, when it was Bobby that served, went to Afghanistan and came back a little quieter and a lot more broken than when he left. The only thing that stayed the same was his loyalty to his old friend, good ole Tommy.

I put up with him because he's friends with Brandon and Jason, but if it was my choice, I wouldn't have him on my team. I guess that means I should be thankful he didn't scrape through boot camp and make any sort of rank. He's the type of guy you'd shoot yourself before relying on him having your back in a firefight, and I told him that one exceptionally whiney day last year. God's honest truth, there's only been one other person I've ever told that to, and she'd just spent 6 hours digging a foxhole with me. That one made it through boot camp, but she didn't make it past AIT—which is a good thing. Just thinking about that one driving a tractor trailer full of missiles scared the crap out of me. Something about a threesome in a hotel room, a couple of X-rated Polaroids, and a very homophobic pre-don't ask, don't tell Army. Some people have no sense, but in her case, I think she knew exactly what she was doing. She wanted out of her contract and let her drill sergeant "discover" those pics in her locker during an inspection. Tommy, I think, would have been one of those types that would drop a grenade, scream like a little girl and end up blowing everyone up around him while he ran for the hills.

"Roxy, please come play referee here," KL said.

Brandon and KL were arguing. I rolled my eyes and made a mental reminder to stay on point.

"We need to go find him, we've got time." Brandon directed that at both of us.

"For now. But if he is hiding under a table or something I am going to whip his scrawny butt." KL's jaw thrust out stubbornly leaving deep grooves on each side of her mouth, but it was her fists I was worried about. Leather creaked along her palm where her bracer ended. Only her fingers and thumb were exposed, but she wasn't using them to point or make her favorite gesture. I cocked my head and smiled, then waded in between the two of them before it got ugly.

"Bobby, why don't you take us to the last place you two were together and we will go from there." Then I turned to my wife. "We are going to stick together, for now."

"Why can't we just get out of here? We need to get home. We have no idea what is happening there." From the tone of her voice, I could tell she was starting to dig her heels in.

"Because right now there's safety in numbers." When in doubt use logic, that's my motto when dealing with KL. It doesn't always work, but it's better than trying to bully her. That's a sure fire way to be on the wrong end of a mental game of tug-of-war.

"Fine," she muttered, then stalked away to join the group.

Great. KL is pissed, we don't know what the hell is happening and we're all traipsing around a human funfetti filled convention center looking for someone who was probably not worth looking for. I was just starting to get a bad feeling about the whole thing when KL started to laugh. Paul joined in, holding his fist under his nose to hold in the laughter. Someone snorted, then everyone just stopped in front of me.

"What the heck, people?" Being short was a pain in the ass most days. Being short in a group of people who were ALL taller than me was downright annoying, especially when they were blocking my view. The elbows came out, and our little group parted in front of me out of deference to a bruised pair of ribs rather than my queen-like stature.

"Move. Get out of the way."

KL was the last one blocking my view. Evidently, she had lost the power of speech because she just grinned and pointed toward the escalators before dramatically sweeping her coat aside to let me pass.

"Holy shit." That was the best I could do— other than pinching my lips together to keep myself from giggling like a madwoman. The escalators were still moving, just like everything else electrical in the convention center, but the people weren't...which meant when everything human stopped, they just kept on going all the way to the bottom.

Everyone from Spiderman to the Hulk were toppled over at the bottom of the down escalator, all piled on top of each other while the escalator stairs continued their endless circular march around and around. It looked like some kid's entire superhero collection had been tossed down a laundry chute into some strange alternate reality. Suddenly, I felt very small.

That didn't fuck with my brain one bit, nope.

For a second I wasn't sure if we weren't all toys and I was just imagining the whole thing. I even looked up to make sure the roof wasn't missing on one side and we weren't standing inside a huge dollhouse. "I swear to God, if I see a giant pair of eyes staring down at me, or I find a giant pile of kiddy snot somewhere, I will totally freak out on all of you."

KL caught my drift instantly. A sly expression came over her face and an evil glint shone in her eyes. She leaned closer to me and whispered.

"You know...if you're right, that means Brandon has nothing going on down there beneath those camo pants," she paused and made a rude gesture before drawling, "nothing but smooth plastic."

Sometimes all you can do is shake your head, admit that you married someone with a very warped sense of humor, and carry on. That sounded like a good option today, although I had to admit it was funny and it helped with the heebie-jeebies. I reached out and gave her hand a quick squeeze. "Thanks, babe. I needed that."

"Anytime." She squeezed back, then turned her attention back to the group. "Bobby? Where'd you last see Tommy, dude?"

"That way," Bobby said, pointing towards a row of tables sitting next to the elevator.

"Not upstairs?" KL asked, glancing nervously at the elevator then back towards the escalator.

She hated elevators. Actually, it was more than that. She hated elevators with a phobia like intensity, enough to give them a nickname: plunging death boxes to hell. If Bobby was suggesting a ride on an elevator now, he was going to be sorely disappointed. It was hard enough to get her to go inside one at the best of times, it would take rope, an act of God, and maybe a tranquilizer to accomplish that feat right now. Weird shit had a tendency to make people squirrelly and KL was no exception.

"No." Bobby stopped right in front of a dense group of mannequin people clustered in front of a table covered in box after box of old comic books. "We were right here when everyone froze."

"Okay. Everyone spread out and look for him."

KL had already wandered away and was lifting up tablecloths to peer under them, using the sword cane like a snake stick and keeping her distance from the covered tables. When she caught me watching her, she grinned at me without a single ounce of shame and shrugged. "What? I figure if he was anywhere, he'd be cowering somewhere out of sight."

"I'm not saying a word." I returned the smile with my own, nodding wryly at her more than accurate expectation before beginning my own table-tent inspection in the other direction. If anyone would have chosen to go to ground like a wounded gopher, it was him.

"Tommy? Tommy?" Bobby started calling out for his friend, then Ann and Brandon joined in.

"Really?" I hissed, marching up to Bobby and glaring at him. "You really want to be that loud in here? There's other people out there. Not many, but enough...all scurrying around like rats in a garbage dump. How many rats in one group would it take to make them bold enough to challenge us? Do you really want to deal with other people? Potentially hostile people?"

"No. I guess not," Bobby muttered.

Bobby ducked his head in apology before slipping away again. The Tommy's continued, but now they were choked, half-whispered attempts with a seriously annoying sibilant quality. Three deeper male voices and two higher female one's participating in a really screwed up acapella version of hide and go seek.

I stalked away before something inside my head exploded. In the end, KL was right. We found him crouched in a corner, half hidden behind a trashcan and a pile of empty cardboard boxes. In his excitement, Bobby rushed over and shook him. Maybe he thought Tommy was asleep, or maybe just playing possum while he waited for someone to come rescue him, but Tommy wasn't doing any of that. He just toppled over, frozen into position and as still as the rest of them.

"That makes no sense at all," KL said, hunkering down next to the two men.

"What doesn't?" Brandon asked her.

"He looks like he froze after everyone else. Look, he made it all the way over to the corner here. He's not just standing like the rest of them. He had time to crouch down and hide, and look at his face."

Tommy's face was a frozen mask of fear. His teeth were bared and his lips were drawn back as if he had frozen in mid-scream, but it was his eyes that freaked me out the most. Usually, you could see fear in someone's eyes, a glaze of emotion that only exists in the living. It was a subtle thing that we all recognized, even if we never consciously thought about it.

Ever look at a photo and without knowing anything else about the person in it you can tell that they're dead, as in for real, dead? It's like that. There's just something animated inside human eyes that lets you know someone's home inside. Tommy's eyes didn't reflect the fear in his face. They weren't dead either. Dead eyes lost the ability to see, the pupils dilating as the darkness found them.

I reached down and pulled back Tommy's eyelids to get a better look. The pupils were still constricted, but they didn't react to changes in the light around him either. I shuddered. They weren't dead eyes, they were doll's eyes and that was somehow worse.

"Bobby, you said you were together, then everyone froze and he was gone?"

He nodded.

"Huh." So Tommy hadn't frozen right away. My thoughts returned to the rent-a-cop we had found earlier and wondered if that was what had happened to him. But, if he had frozen, hot dog or not...he wouldn't have choked and died. My head was starting to hurt. There was too many variables and not enough answers.

"What the hell is that?" Lauren asked, thankfully interrupting my train of thought.

A low humming sound was coming from somewhere. Bobby hadn't left his friends side yet. He leaned closer, twisting his head so he could hear better, and looked up at us.

"It's coming from Tommy!" he exclaimed. Wide eyed with excitement, he shook his friend, then slapped his face. "C'mon buddy. Wake up. Wake up, Tommy!"

He was rocking Tommy in his arms now, his voice getting louder and higher with each repetition. He looked up, searching each face around him with a sort of desperation I'd seen before, back during my emergency response days. That wild eyed look that somehow managed to combine despair and hope in a gut twisting human response to newly minted death. "Guys? KL? Why won't he wake up? He's trying to talk. Don't you hear him?"

We all stepped back and exchanged glances. No one seemed to know what to say. Then Brandon cocked his head and turned around in a slow circle. "Uh, guys?"

Such a small voice coming from Brandon was enough to grab my attention. My heart sped up and I had to pee again courtesy of that good ole' flight or fight response. Gotta love the way us humans are hardwired.

"What?" I snapped.

"Tommy's not the only one humming."

KL

Brandon was right. All the frozen people were emitting a low groan. It was so low it hadn't even registered until he pointed it out, sort of like having to pet a cat before you realized it was purring. Except this noise wasn't relaxing like a cat's purr. It skated across your nerves with an eerie edge that felt like it was shaving off a layer of dead skin. Goosebumps crawled up my arms and sent every hair on the back of my neck reaching for the sky.

"Okay, people. We need to leave—now," Roxy said, pulling out her best drill sergeant voice. There wasn't going to be any room for discussion, not anymore. "This little game of find the missing group member is done. Over." Her expression was about as hard as I've seen it, right down to the small muscle that always jumped at the corner of her jaw from clenching it too hard. She made a sharp cutting motion with her hand, then basically gave Bobby the palm when he tried to argue. "No. No more."

"But..." Bobby stuttered, looking about as forlorn as a child whose shitty stepdad just sold his puppy for a case of beer. It wasn't that I didn't have any sympathy for the poor sap, I just couldn't see any way to fix what was going on and we were running out of options. I stepped up and took over before Roxy went full on despot on these fools.

"Look. Tommy's a lost cause, and in case you haven't noticed it, Jason hasn't waltzed his happy ass back in here to tell us everything is roses and champagne outside of those doors either. He's either baled on us or done what Tommy did and froze up after everyone else. For all I know, he's somewhere out there, and about as effective as a giant size GI Joe doll by now. I'm not sticking around to see if we might be next. Are you?" I asked, staring down each and every one of them in turn. It wasn't quite fair, that fight. It's hard to win a staring contest when the other person is wearing shades, that person being me. All they see is their own distorted face in reflective black, while I catch every tick and twitch that signifies weakness.

Paul pulled Lauren close to him and, after checking with her, nodded agreement for the both of them. I gave them a thumbs up. Lauren would always have our back, and where Lauren went, Paul followed. That was two out of four falling into line right away, and that wasn't bad.

Ann stepped up. Somewhere in this maze of commercial crap and stiff bodies she had found, of all things, an honest to goodness shepherds crook. One of those 5 foot tall wooden staffs shaped like a question mark that, with a little creativity, would make a great combat stave. My opinion of her jumped a few marks, even if she did look like a rainbow colored Little Bo Peep standing there in cotton candy pink shoes that I swore she dyed to match the hair.

"I don't know what's going on, but I trust you. If you say we should leave, I say we should leave." Those were brave words coming from a woman that didn't even know us and I think she managed to shame Bobby and Brandon. Their cheeks colored and they even looked a little embarrassed.

"Fine. I get it," Brandon muttered. He crouched down next to Bobby and gave him a good, long, hard look before carefully reaching out to pat his shoulder. "Dude. We've got to go. You've got to leave Tommy here, bud. I know you don't want to but there isn't anything we can do for him."

Bobby sniffled and wiped his nose with his sleeve, then he stood up.

"Good man." Brandon patted his shoulders robustly, then shook him until he looked up. "You good? You can't help Tommy but the rest of us need you."

"I'm good," Bobby said, taking a huge breath in and then out. His demeanor changed. He straightened up until he was practically standing at attention, his jaw set perfectly horizontal to the floor and his eyes clearer than I'd ever seen them before. Before he moved into line, he cast a quick glance in my direction and tossed a quick two finger salute towards me. I didn't know what else to do, so I just nodded. Roxy's the one with military training, not

59

me…but if that meant he'd follow us without arguing I'd take it.

"Let's go." We were ready to boogie the hell out of here.

Everything was going well until I saw daylight. The weird humming noise continued but it was hard to remember it was there when you were busy staring at every face you passed. My paranoia was running high again and I could feel my heart thudding against my breastbone and I had to keep loosening my grip on the sword cane handle. Everything was going too well. We almost made it all the way through to the front of the exhibition room when it happened.

Roxy sneezed. Not a little tiny girly sneeze either. Nope, this was a shake the rafters sneeze.

My head snapped around. "Seriously?"

"It's not my fault. It's not like I can control when a sneeze is going to happen. Besides, some of these guys have on way too much cologne. It's like walking through Macy's and getting crop-dusted by perfume girls." Roxy punched one of the mannequin people in the arm hard enough to make him wobble. A tall man dressed to the nines in something overly lacey and Victorian, she plucked a fancy handkerchief out of his velveteen coat pocket and blew her nose. "I wish someone would tell people not to bathe in the stuff, that's what water…is…um, for?" Roxy stuttered to a stop, her rant turning into a question that had nothing to do with the subject at hand but had everything to do with what was going on around us.

The low hum had stopped.

A dozen heads turned toward us with all the mechanical sluggishness of a music box dancer, surrendering their mannequin like immobility, and were now staring at us...unblinking. "That is so creepy."

"No, that is beyond creepy. Let's get the hell out of here." Roxy started walking faster.

As if pulled along by the strings of our accelerated exit, several of the mannequins found their feet. They started shuffling behind us, a slow progression that followed our movements. They focused on us with a strange intensity that made petting a rabid dog sound safer than letting a single one of them within arms distance of us. I was hesitant to call them zombies, even in my own head, but gazing into those cold, cold eyes and seeing nothing remotely human inside them? I really had no choice. I wasn't ready to utter the word out loud. That would make what had always been fantasy, a twisted apocalyptic tale that had found its way into graphic novels and onto the big screen, and turned it into something real.

These weren't plastic bobble heads dancing on the dashboards of tricked out SUV's. These were living, breathing human beings, or had been, and now they were something else. We had created the modern zombie out of nothing but myth and imagination, the overly caffeinated neurons of sleepless writers and artists armed with pens and paper. We named them and gave them a place in our fictional iconography, simultaneously reassuring the masses that zombies could never exist in the real world while effectively feeding our need to be frightened for entertainment. Well, space travel and laser beams had been the stuff of science fiction at one time, so why not zombies? It was irony at its best, and we were the butt of some great cosmic joke.

I wanted to burst out laughing at the madness of it all, but there wasn't time. I drew out the sword, more prepared to use it than I expected, and backed up to Roxy. There was no way in hell I was going to let one of those things get near us. They would have to get through me to get to her.

"Move it. Get to the doors. Come on!" somebody bellowed, and we all took off towards the hall entrance. The awkward sound of poorly landing feet slapping against the linoleum picked up behind us. Looking back was a mistake. What I saw behind us lit a fire under my ass. A horde of costumed zombies lurched toward us with all the grace of, well, a horde of zombies. I almost tripped over my own feet dancing in a quick circle while still trying to maintain forward momentum.

That brought me to Rule Number 3 when dealing with zombies: Deep thoughts on the how's and why's of a zombie apocalypse are all good and well— when you have time and a safe place to think about them—otherwise they are a distraction that might get you killed.

We barely made it through the doors before the horde reached us. I kicked out one door stopper and Bobby managed to toe out the other one, but it was the damn hydraulics that almost got us killed. The doors weren't designed to be slammed shut, nope...they had to release slowly, just in case someone's kid decided to play with the gap between the hinges or stand in the middle so they could get their fingers caught. What was meant to be a safety feature almost got us killed as we pushed against the doors, trying to get them to close faster. My arms strained against the metered pace, but they weren't budging.

One of them made it to the door before it shut all the way. A wild haired man shorter than me by about 4 inches, with a cigar still drooping out of the corner of his mouth swiped out at me with plastic claws.

"Goddammit!" I yelled. This day was really testing my limits if how many times I've had to curse was an indicator.

My hands were full so I used what I had. Even in the midst of all the insanity, a part of my brain registered the cheap wife beater tee and faded jeans, the familiar two day old beard and shaved lip, and I almost lost it. I was being attacked by a freaking mini-me version of Wolverine. He only weighed about a buck-twenty soaking wet, tops, but he was fast. I landed the toe of one of my black leather engineer boots right smack dap into his solar plexus. It didn't drop him and a sweet spot shot like that should have emptied his lungs out like a punctured balloon. It didn't. Hell, he didn't even register the kick, but it did bowl him back into the crowd and give me enough time to close the door. A second later the doors shook with multiple impacts, a dozen or more zombies hammered against the heavy steel but not a one figured out how to work the door handles. Interesting.

Lauren showed up with a length of red rope, the kind they used to keep everyone in line with, and started tying the two doors together. The doors rattled again. We both jumped but managed to get a good knot in before heading for Paul and Brandon, who were clinging to the other two sets of doors for dear life, digging their heels into the crappy blue and red ticked carpeting and yelling for Lauren to hurry up. Well, Brandon was yelling at Lauren. Paul was yelling at Brandon to shut the hell up and stop yelling at Lauren. I noticed Paul got his door tied first. Roxy snorted and turned her back on them, she had noticed where the lines were being drawn, too. A subtle hierarchy was slowly developing inside our little group that didn't bode well for Brandon. Being on the bottom of the zombie apocalypse food chain meant you were being voted most likely to turn into zombie bait. I got a feeling from Lauren's expression that Brandon's likelihood of survival just dropped a notch. She didn't like being yelled at.

"Is everybody okay?" Paul asked.

I found a folding chair and plopped down into it. "As opposed to what, Paul?"

"Well, I mean, no one got bit or anything, did they?"

That question kept us busy for a few minutes, but after a thorough once over, we discovered we had all miraculously escaped unscathed, except for me. I had broken a damn nail.

"What now? The trucks are out in the back by the loading docks, we're stuck in here and there's crap loads, of what? Honest to God Zombies behind that door and between us and our way home."

That was it. Somebody actually said it, now it was all too real. I saw a couple of faces blanch at the word. The one's who didn't react badly, you can bet had already been thinking it. They just didn't want to be the first ones to suggest it.

"Zombies?" Brandon piped up. "We don't know they're zombies. I mean, this is just a game, play acting like in the movies. They aren't like, for real, are they? They can't be."

Brandon sounded unsure of himself, but he had a good question. We still didn't know what we were dealing with. Yeah, we were calling them zombies, but did that mean they did everything that zombies did? Were they undead? Infected with something? If they bit you would you catch it and turn into a zombie too?

So many questions.

"I don't know, feel free to go back out there and try to question them, but don't expect an answer," I said.

The main courtyard of the convention center was empty, devoid of any other life moving or otherwise, other than us. Most of the convention goer's had already gone inside the hall when everything went to hell. The only people left out here would have been the ticket takers and the cops sitting in front and checking for weapons. Everything we had brought in, all of the plastic guns, swords and miscellaneous weapon like items had been inspected and a little orange sticker placed on them to show they were safe. I was surprised the sword cane had made it through, but the prior owner had altered it so much the poor cops probably didn't have a clue how it opened. Finding it had given me hope that there was more "oops" snuck in here and there, but so far our search had been futile. Making it this far got me thinking.

"Hey, Hun? Can you come here for a sec?"

"What's up?" Roxy asked. I pulled her aside, out of earshot of the boys.

"Do you remember where those cops were stationed? The real ones, not the rent a cops?"

"Yeah?" she asked, then it struck her. Weapons. Real ones.

"Exactly." I grinned.

Roxy narrowed her eyes and scanned the area around them. "I want those gun belts. If they're here we need to find them. First."

"I agree."

"And if there are any more of those...things out here, we need to know." She waived her hand towards the doors. The pounding had slowed down to a slow bass beat that had zero rhythm. The steel doors had held up well and for now, we seemed safe. It was time to make sure we stayed that way.

"Hey guys? We're going to do a little recon. See if we can find a safe exit and get out of here."

"That sounds like a good idea, maybe we can find Jason." Brandon jumped up, ready to get on the move again.

I did not want him following us. The cops had been off to the left, so we sent Brandon and Bobby off to the right and Paul stayed with Ann and Lauren.

Before we left, I tapped Paul on the shoulder. "Hey, man. If anything, ANY THING, changes or happens while we're gone, whistle and we'll come running, okay?"

"Right. Be safe."

"Sure," I said, sounding way more chipper than I ought to.

We headed out and made it about 20 yards when Roxy went on point like a hound on a scent trail and stalked over to a cloth covered table. The tablecloth came off in one dramatic yank that almost managed to look like one of the table tricks where the magician pulls off the tablecloth and all the stuff on it stays put. Except nothing stayed put and it rained flyers all over the place.

"What the hell was that all about?" I asked.

"I heard something."

"You're getting jumpy, I'm sure it's nothing," I started to say, then heard it myself. A scurrying noise, much like a rat but a lot bigger. I yanked back another tablecloth but this time the table tumbled over with it, trapping our little rat against the underside.

"Oh, my God, it's a kid!" Roxy exclaimed.

"Hey little person, what is your name?" I hunkered down and asked in my best 'come here I won't bite' voice. In other words, I was trying to sound friendly.

"She's not a puppy or kitten," Roxy drawled, evidently perfectly happy to stand by and watch my comedic attempts at child wrangling.

The little girl's eyes were as huge as saucers and she whimpered a little when Roxy came closer. Then she looked at me and her eyes managed to get even wider. "You're the Revenant Chaser!" she said, going from scared to excited in less than a second. "My brother has your comic books. He doesn't let me read them but I do anyway."

Roxy chuckled and I ignored her. "That's right."

Whatever worked, right?

"Cool!" she exclaimed, then pointed behind us. "Are you going to kill all the Soulless and save everyone?"

"What?" I looked behind me. "Oh, shit."

There was no time to run. I spun around, sword at the ready to meet the zombie lurching towards us, I had every intention of taking the damn things head off.

"Stop. Stop! Don't hurt me!" The zombie yelled, skidding to a halt at my feet. She, I could tell it was a she by her costume, reached up and started pulling at the wounds on her face and tossing pieces of flesh on the ground. "It's not real, see? It's just make-up. I'm one of the volunteer zombies from upstairs," she sobbed.

"Jesus Christ, woman. I almost took your head off," I growled, then lowered my sword.

"Why were you running?" Roxy asked. She had the kid in tow and was staring at the woman cowering at my feet.

"Good question." Leave it to my wife to get straight to it. Unfortunately, the woman never had a chance to answer, not completely. She twisted around and tried to crawl behind us about the same time we looked up and saw what she had been running from.

"Fuck." There wasn't another word to justify what was about to happen. "The food court. We forgot about the food courts."

The convention center had two very crappy grease pits on either side of the hall. They were open on both sides and we had forgotten all about them. Now we had zombies in paper aprons and hairnets, smelling of old fry grease and cheap pizza, all heading our way. I doubt they wanted to take our order.

"Run. Run now," Roxy said.

We ran.

Roxy

The sight of a dozen enraged zombies coming at us was enough to light a fire under anyone's ass. "Where the fuck did they come from?" I gasped, my legs pumping as fast as they could go.

"Don't care." KL kept her eyes straight ahead of her. She was a faster runner than me and I had the extra weight of the kid, but she made sure I didn't fall back.

"What about her?" I didn't have enough air in my lungs to waste explaining who "her" was, but KL got it.

"Don't care," she answered, looking pretty damn grim about it but not slowing down one bit, either.

I heard a scream and suddenly we weren't being pursued anymore. I slowed down, mostly because I needed to, and partly because I had to look. I was pretty much lugging around a child sized sack of grain in my arms that was grinning at us like this was some human roller coaster ride and she was having the time of her life. I had a stitch from hell digging into my ribs and every breath sent a hot poker searing through my lungs. It was a struggle, but KL had the sword so I couldn't pass her off.

Looking back when you know you shouldn't? Now that was just plain human curiosity. They always say that curiosity killed the cat, but people were worse. Much worse. All you have to do is watch the evening news to prove it. We love a good story and the gorier the better. Train wrecks? Forest fires? Perhaps a double homicide in the bad part of town with some juicy side story to give it that extra Jerry Springer appeal? We want it all, and if we lucked out to be right there in the thick of things, as in happening live now? That was all the better.

We've all been stuck in traffic for miles, crawling at the pace of a snail, all because the lookie-loo's must have their moment of titillation. All those otherwise solid citizens rubber necking past the scene of an accident in the hopes of glimpsing a streak of blood, or better yet, bits and pieces of what used to be a human being. The same goes for auto racing. I dare anyone to say they don't watch a bunch of cars circling the same track a hundred times in the hopes of seeing someone wreck. Actually going to a race is like adrenaline laced crack you inhale through the smoke and smell of burning tires and fuel flung across the track like baptismal water. With everything going on right now I was starting to understand the mentality of diehard race fans. Root for your team and to hell with the rest of them. As long as your car made it across the finish line, utter devastation could be left in your wake and it wouldn't matter.

So, I looked...and then I wish I hadn't. The zombies had stopped coming at us because they had found something interesting to play with. Our make believe zombie was on the ground, fighting off a dozen zombies that crawled all over her like giant catfish fighting over Purina catfish chow in a manmade amusement park pond. She never had a chance. Hell, I wasn't even sure she had ever made it to her feet before the zombies reached her.

They started ripping at her, pulling off great chunks of her makeup. Our makeup artist was good at what she did, the realistic moulage pieces had needed a good bit of spirit gum adhesive to stay put and it was not coming off easily. Then one of the zombies got ahold of the bright red wound edges and started peeling off the fake skin. Once they got a good size piece pulled off they started shoveling the rubber into their mouths. The resultant sound was akin to a pack of hounds chewing on rubber squeaky toys, and if it wasn't so horrifying to watch, it would have been funny.

The whole episode looked like some sick freshman zombie orientation, a practice run to help teach them what to do. Evidently, these zombies hadn't received a "How to be a Zombie" instruction manual, they were doing as much damage to themselves and each other as they were to one of the living.

Then one of them managed to hit live flesh and the sharp metallic smell of hot blood hit us and sent them into a feeding frenzy. What happened next was enough to almost make me gag. I pulled the little girl closer to me, hiding her face from the worst of the carnage. She seemed to think this was all a game, but if she changed her mind, a terrified child was prone to yelling and screaming. That would so not be good right now.

KL took one look at her, then at me and the kid. I saw her frown, as if she was reconsidering her prior mercenary decision, but then her face hardened again. She grabbed my sleeve and whispered, "I can't do anything for her now. We need to find the others and warn them."

KL pulled her sword out slowly then backed away even slower. She made the right call. More zombies were descending on the screams and if she had tried to help, well I don't want to think of what would have happened.

"You lead the way. I've got her, you just keep us safe." I'd never been happier that KL had a thing for sharp pointy objects. Sure, it all started off as a character study for the Revenant Chaser, but then it branched off into live appearances. We learned pretty quickly that in order to sell the character it helped if you actually looked like you knew what you were doing. The best way to do that was by actually knowing what you were doing. After several years of training with a martial arts expert, I could trust her not to stab either of us by accident, but if you were the unfortunate soul on the receiving end of anything steel she had her hands on? It was going to get messy.

The front escalators were just behind our backs, the steady click clack of the mechanical stairs hid the sound of our boots scuffing across the carpeting, while the polished metal wall beneath it made for good cover. Unlike the back escalators, these were clear of human debris, moving or otherwise. That worried me. Either no one was taking a ride when all this started, or there was another pocket of zombies to worry about nearby.

"That way," I said, pointing to the gap between the up and down escalators. The minute we were out of line of sight, we turned and ran like hell.

We almost made it back to where we had left Ann and Lauren when we ran into Brandon and Bobby, literally. They were coming from the opposite direction and were hauling ass as fast as we were. Brandon was in full panic mode, outpacing Bobby by a good twenty feet. He was so worried about what was behind him that he didn't see KL and ran full force into her. They both went down in a tangled mess and KL lost her sword. It bounced across the floor and landed a few feet away.

"Dammit, Brandon, watch where you're going," KL growled. I'm not sure if it was intentional or not, but when they both got back up he was cupping his nut-sack. The way she was smiling I would have to say it was deliberate.

"What the hell!" Brandon wheezed while still down on his knees. Then he looked up. "You have a kid?"

"No time to explain," KL said. "We forgot the food court. We need to get the hell out of here now."

"We can't go that way either," Bobby said, pointing back the way they came from.

"That's just great," KL didn't even try to hide her sarcasm. "Food courts, plural. There's one on either side and we're trapped right smack dab in the middle of this shit show."

"Fuck. I refuse to die in this building. There has to be a way out." Okay so that might have come out sounding a bit melodramatic. "Does anyone know where the hell Ann and Lauren are?"

"I don't know. We left them over there with Paul," Brandon said. The deep burgundy ropes we had tied to the doors were still intact. They hadn't gone back inside, so where were they?

"Holy fuck. What the hell is that?" KL's exclamation got everyone's attentions.

Coming straight at us was a flaming zombie, as in, straight on zombie flambeau. Arms waving wildly, it stumbled and spun around while it burned from the waist up. Skin crackled and popped from the fat being ignited but you could still identify enough of their uniform to see who or what it used to be. The blue and white clothing was already familiar. Every single food court worker wore the same ugly outfit, and this one must have been manning the fryer because the horrendous combined odor of chicken wings, french fries and barbequed people screamed grease fire.

"I am so not eating fried food ever again," I muttered beneath my breath, discovering something new about fighting zombies that no one ever discusses. Zombies are a great for the diet. Between the ick factor and the smell, I wasn't sure if I ever wanted to eat again.

The little girl caught sight of our very own burning man and started screaming in my arms. I couldn't blame her but damn it was loud. She was squirming so badly I had to let her go before she fell. She ran for the nearest table and crawled underneath it. That was one smart kiddie there. If we got out of here, I might even remember to ask her name or find out where her parents were.

KL cast around for her sword, but Brandon snatched it up before she could get to it. "Hey give it back. Roxy stole it first. It's mine now."

"Hell no! You put it down, it's mine now."

KL's face darkened, and she advanced on Brandon. "No, it's not."

"Uh. Guys..." I reminded them. "We've got other problems right now." In addition to Flambeau, we had a second zombie coming our way. I had managed to keep the baton tucked into my belt, and with the kid in hiding I finally had my hands free.

Eight pounds of pressure, that's all it takes...I kept reminding myself, that's enough to crack a skull open. Someone was about to get brained because I was not going to end up zombie bait. A few loose practice swings, and I was ready.

KL gave him one last disgusted look, then found something else she could use. Flambeau was extinguished in a cloud of white dust and was reduced to a smoking mess that didn't slow them down. A solid metal cylinder aimed at its head did. The nozzle whipped around like a black snake, but it was the solid ting of steel on skull that carried the real bite. Tiny flakes of burnt skin flew all over the place, and I tried really hard not to think about what the other bits of white and pink were made of. Chest heaving from the effort, KL didn't wait to see if it would get back up. She swung again, and this time she had the floor beneath her to work with. Its head exploded like a clove of garlic beneath a kitchen mallet.

Brandon swung KL's sword in a wide arc and yelled. Not just any yell, either. It was a full on, worthy of any Xena episode battle cry. In he went through the dusty cloud left over by the fire extinguisher, still making too much noise and slashing wildly at anything and nothing in front of him.

We could hear more footsteps running toward us, but we couldn't see through the haze yet. We heard breathing, a few curses and then Ann stepped through the rapidly dissipating smoke. Flambeau might have been extinguished, but he hadn't given up smoking yet. Bobby was standing over the second zombie with a huge knife in his hand. He looked up at us with a pleased expression on his face, then leaned over and wiped the blood off his blade with the dead zombies' shirt. Unlike the rest of us, he appeared rather nonplussed about the whole thing. He wasn't even breathing heavily. I had a feeling Bobby was in his element now, and that was a little bit scary.

"Where the hell did he get a big ass knife like that?" KL muttered. She was still peeved about the no weapons rule.

"Hell if I know, but I'm glad he had it." For all I knew he had it hidden somewhere on his person this whole time. That would be something he'd pull. He was way more paranoid than all the rest of put together. He also didn't let on that he had it until it was absolutely necessary and that was like him, as well. He never looked for a fight, but if it came to him, the scary would come out. God help the fool who thought because Bobby was quiet that he was easy pickings.

I did a quick check for anymore zombies but we were in the clear. The little girl was still hiding under the tables and was refusing to come out.

"Freaking douchebag," KL muttered angrily.

I groaned and straightened up from my futile attempts at getting the little girl to trust me again.

KL might have been able to do it, but one look at her face told me she wasn't in the right mood for kiddy lassoing. In fact, she looked downright pissed. Brandon was standing next to Bobby, patting him on the back and poking at the dead zombie with KL's sword. He reminded me of the folks who used to take credit for someone else's work, simply because they were in charge of a project.

Ann joined us. She looked at KL's face then over at the boys. "Oh, boy," she said. "Isn't that your sword?"

"Yeah."

"Huh." Ann pursed her lips as if she was considering something important, then nodded her head. She handed KL her shepherd's staff. "Can you hold this for me? I'll take care of the little girl. I've got a niece her age."

"Okay, sure."

Paul stepped up. Lauren was hugging him tightly, but it was hard to tell who was holding up who. They looked pretty rough, but no one had any blood on them so I was happy.

"You know Brandon had a chance to take out that zombie. He froze at the last second. It's a good thing Bobby was right behind him or he would have been toast," Lauren admitted.

"Really?" KL drawled. Her eyes narrowed dangerously. She hadn't really been asking, you could tell by the tone of her voice. What I heard was gears spinning while she tried to decide what to do about that little piece of knowledge.

"Brandon?" KL called out, her voice was deceptively mellow. She held her hand out, palm up and gestured with her fingers. "I need my sword back now."

"You set it down, that made it fair game," Brandon said, resting the sword on his shoulder like a baseball bat. KL shook her head, obviously disappointed in his answer.

"I'm only going to give you one warning. Give me my sword back now." KL closed in on Brandon, idly twirling the staff as she walked. Lauren looked at me and I shrugged. This wasn't going to be pretty.

"Bobby?" Brandon stepped closer to his friend. He didn't look nervous until Bobby gave him a disgusted look and stepped away.

"Someone needs to stand watch," Bobby said, nodding at us before walking away. He wasn't even going to watch the show.

"Wrong answer." KL swung the staff and used the crook to hook him behind the knee. One pull and he was down.

She snatched her sword up and held it right to his throat. He swallowed, and the blade came in contact with his skin. A bright red spot popped up on his neck and he froze, sweating his fear out along his forehead. He smelled like a coward. "Never touch my sword again."

Evidently, KL was done being nice.

"Thank you, Ann," KL offered her the staff back.

I guess I was wrong. That was actually nice of her.

"My hands are full," Ann said. She had managed to coax the little girl out of her hiding place and was now carrying her on her hip. "Everyone, this is Carol Ann."

A chorus of hello's met her announcement and the little girl, Carol Ann, smiled and waved her hand at them all.

"I'll take it," Brandon croaked. We all turned and stared at him. He was busy dabbing at his neck and acting like he'd been mortally wounded.

"No. I will." Paul took the staff before Brandon could get his hands on it. Brandon shot daggers at KL and looked like he was going to make an issue of it.

"Get over yourself, Brandon, I've seen worse razor cuts than that. Paul gets the staff, he has Lauren to worry about, at least until she finds her own weapon."

That was said with a quick nod towards Lauren. I was so not the type that expected the men to be the hero protecting the damsel in distress and they all knew that. We also knew that Lauren was as tough as nails and could hold her own, but we only had so many weapons between us. Paul would fend off an army of zombies to keep her safe, and that meant one less person to worry about.

The background music being pumped through the speakers suddenly stopped, replaced by an incoherent squelch loud enough to make my ears bleed.

"Ow, what the fuck?" KL visibly flinched. She had sensitive ears that rarely missed anything. She swore she could hear a grasshopper pass gas in the middle of the night and I believed her.

A disembodied voice followed another loud squelch, broadcasting throughout the entire building. "Guys, stop messing around. Go through the door on your left and head down the hallway. There's another set of elevators up ahead. Take them to the third floor."

We stood there, staring at each other like idiots, until the voice sounded off again...this time more urgently.

"Come on people. If you want to live, you need to start hauling ass."

"Is that...?" Lauren asked.

"Yeah, I think it is, and I think we should listen to him." KL turned and bellowed. "Bobby, get your ass back here. We're moving on up."

KL

No one had any time to ask how Jason knew where we were or how he got where he was. We were too busy taking instructions and trying to look in all four directions at once while we navigated a maze of offices and store rooms. At this point it was run from one room to another, rest for a minute then run again.

There were nerve racking periods of silence where we didn't get any information and we had to guess which way to go. Then we'd hear from Jason again, his disembodied voice guiding us over the loudspeakers.

"Look for the cameras, people." Jason's voice intruded on our little party again.

"Well, that just made too much freaking sense," Roxy grumbled, pointing up at the small cylindrical camera set into the wall above us.

"Really, Jason? Now you tell us?" I knew he couldn't hear us, but he could see us, so I communicated with him the only way I knew how. I got as close to the camera as I could and threw up both arms and gave him the ole KL salute. "Asshole."

"Back at you, buddy. But if I were you, I'd get moving again. You all are almost there."

"He's not telling us something." Jason's banter had sounded strained but I couldn't ask him a damn thing. This one-way conversation was for the birds.

"Maybe, but do we have a choice?"

There was always a choice. But, before I could think of one, we were at our destination.

Paul pushed the button to go up while we all crowded around. The elevator light popped on and we all looked up. The damn thing was on the third floor. The clink and pop of ancient machinery grumbled awake, and I tried really hard not to think about the empty vertical chute just on the other side of those metal doors. Every noise sounded like the wheeze of an ancient machine that was 10 seconds away from rattling apart. As far as I was concerned elevators should have a more appropriate name. Metal boxes of death seemed a more fitting description. Did I mention I hated elevators?

"Seriously? This has got to be the slowest elevator in the world," Brandon said. His eyes were glued to the little white light.

The elevator made a weak ding noise. It had finally made it to the second floor. The irony of the situation was not lost on me. Not only did I have to go on an elevator but I had to wait for it to get to us. The damn thing was probably programmed to hit every floor.

"Roxy I am not sure about this. Maybe I can just find the stairs and take them instead."

"No, you have no idea what we might encounter in three flights of stairs. Or even where they are."

"But..." I let my anxiety get the best of me.

"Seriously? We are in the middle of a zombie apocalypse and you are going to let an elevator be your breaking point?"

"Fine. But I don't have to like it."

Brandon must have been listening in on our conversation because just then he decided to add his two cents. "Really, KL? Don't be a pussy. It's just an elevator."

Thank you, Brandon, for being a consistent target when I needed one. I turned on him, anger gleefully burning out my anxiety in a flash. "Yeah? I don't think you have any room to talk, Brandon. For someone with a dick, you're more of a pussy than I could ever be. If Bobby hadn't saved your sorry ass back there, you'd be zombie bait right now."

I was still pissed at him for trying to steal my blade, especially since I lost it because he bounced into me in the first place.

Which leads me to Rule Number 4: Don't give up your weapon. Don't lay it down unless absolutely necessary, and if you do lose it, pick it up immediately or else an idiot may get ahold of it.

Brandon's eyes widened considerably and he started looking around him for support. Bobby just grinned at him. Not a nice grin either. There was humor there, but it was a grim, toothy, gallows sort of humor that you expect to see on a wolf. The kind of grin that makes you wonder if they're planning on eating you or just walking up to you and taking a leak on your neck. Paul ignored him and Lauren gave him a disappointed look. Ann was too busy with the little one to care either way, but I'm pretty sure he wasn't winning fan points there either. He didn't even bother looking at Roxy. That was probably for the best.

We were all facing the group and the group was all crowded around the elevator. Brandon was about to say something when the shit hit the fan.

"Duck!" I yelled, raising my sword and racing straight towards Brandon. He squealed and did a pretty good imitation of bending under the limbo stick. I didn't know he was that limber.

Everything slowed down and I stopped hearing anything around me. A million random thoughts rattled through my brain while my body responded instinctively, leveling the sharp blade for a powerful swing that might have just shaved off a few chin hairs on the man. Meanwhile, the laughing person in the far corner of my mind where it stays all cozy and multicolored was asking if there was a phonetic connection between the limbo dance and limber, only to race off into another direction and traverse the theological ramifications of a special waiting room for unbaptized souls to bide their time. Adrenaline was a wonderful drug, but it lacked direction. I needed to focus.

I really have to say that in that moment, Brandon must have honestly believed I had had enough and was going to kill him. The fear in his eyes was gratifying to say the least, but there wasn't any time to savor it. Part of me acknowledged that someone else was saving his ass, again...but he wasn't armed and I was.

The blade bit nicely into a rather stodgy looking woman wearing high heels and a skirt suit. She screamed secretary, except for those fingernails. Over an inch long and garishly painted. Part of me wondered how she typed with those things and the other part winced at the thought of those claws getting ahold of me and digging in. The garishly red fingernails didn't match her outfit, but it sure did match the bright red line of blood that arced away from her when I separated her head from her body. She slid to the ground, knees first, and then tumbled forward onto Brandon's lap. He pushed her away then kept backpedaling until he was flat against the wall next to the elevator.

Sound was coming back to me and it made everything worse. I liked the silence better. Our little charge was crying, Roxy was yelling at Brandon and Lauren was cussing up a storm while she swung her Bug Out bag back and forth to beat off a spindly little middle aged man with a comb over and a severe under bite. Beneath it all was an odd whining noise that reminded me of something, then it hit me. It was the noise you make in your sleep, when

89

you think you're screaming, but all that comes out in the waking world is a high pitched wheeze. It was a horrible sound and it was coming from Brandon. He had curled up in the fetal position right below the control panel and had his hands over his ears.

At least he was out of the way.

I wasn't too sure if Lauren wasn't taking out some past aggression on an old employer from the way she emphasized every swing with a few choice words. Paul stepped in and hooked the bastard and that was when it got messy.

Lauren still had those damn stiletto boots. She had taken them off earlier but had refused to give them up, instead tying the laces together and hanging them off her shoulder with a shrug.

"They're expensive, and my fav's," she had spoken without apology, and now they were coming in handy. She dropped the bug out bag and grabbed her boots, then sunk four inches of stiletto heel into the man's left eye.

"Eww," Lauren said, then bent over and heaved.

I had to agree with her assessment. These zombies, or whatever they were, looked too damn alive. Not at all like the movies. There wasn't some magical transformation that turned them gray skinned and milky eyed, nor were they desiccated things that fell apart easily. These were all juicy fresh and way too alive looking for comfort.

Bobby was busy with his own zombie but I couldn't find Roxy. I heard her but didn't see her. I spun back around to see her slide into home plate, using her body to keep the elevator doors from closing completely. Through the haze of excitement and carnage I hadn't quite caught what she had been yelling, but a quick mental rewind of the last two minutes caught me up.

"Fuck! Get in now," Roxy yelled, pulling herself up and holding the doors open manually. They kept cycling through their open/close cycle but her hands kept them from closing completely. Her nightstick was on the ground. I ran, scooping it up on the way and dived into the dull gray box. Lauren and Paul were right behind me and Bobby took up the rear, taking a few swipes at the next zombie that got too close so Ann could get in with her namesake, Carol Ann.

"Brandon, move it!" I bellowed. Sure, he was a jerk, but he was one of the team and I wouldn't just leave him there. I already had to leave a person behind, and I really didn't want to do it again if I could help it.

He scuttled underneath Roxy's legs and tumbled into the elevator and Roxy spun away from the doors, just in time for a new group of zombies to round the corner.

"Close dammit!" Paul yelled, hitting the buttons frantically. The doors weren't closing. They kept trying and then they would shudder and start to open again, as if holding them open for so long had confused the mechanism. Paul and Bobby leaned against the smooth metal doors and pushed, trying to get them to close. "Crap. They're coming!"

I stepped up, away from the railing I had put a death grip on and aimed low and through the door. "If you're squeamish, I'd look away now," I said, just as the next zombie slammed into the half open doors. This time I wasn't trying for a clean kill. I needed a diversion that would keep the rest of the horde from climbing into this little death box with us. A quick up and over slice did the trick, along with a well-placed high kick. Guts tumbled out, and the smell of hot intestines filled the air.

"Christ, what is that smell?" Ann moaned, covering her mouth and nose.

"Just a little something for the zombies to play slip and slide in," I answered with a grin, just as the doors gave up and closed with a sigh.

I seconded that sigh and sagged against the back wall. I didn't take stock of our raggedy group, all that mattered was that we all made it and that Brandon had finally shut the hell up. I closed my eyes and willed the thing to move faster.

"Why isn't there any music in this place?" I asked, peeved as all get out. "We should at least have some kind of music to kill zombies with."

Roxy shook her head at me and smiled. "This isn't the movies, babe. We don't get a soundtrack."

"Well, that's bullshit." There should be something kick ass playing in the background while you kill zombies.

The elevator dinged and a collective breath was taken and held. We had arrived on the third floor.

Roxy

The elevator doors slid open. Jason was there, waiting for us, excitedly shifting from one booted foot to the other.

"Hey!" His greeting was cut short when Ann stepped forward with Carol Ann in her arms. Pale eyebrows climbed straight up his forehead then back down again. For a big burly guy he was adorably shy around strange woman. We didn't count. KL and I were more like one of the guys and Lauren was taken, but Ann was barely dressed and his eyes went straight for her cleavage before he noticed what she was carrying. "Um, cute kid."

Carol Ann scowled at him, then hid her face in Ann's hair. I didn't blame her. Jason was a good guy, but damn, he had an ugly mug. The man was over six feet tall and probably about two hundred and forty pounds of pure muscle. He was also pale as hell and perpetually sunburned, although that particular shade of red he was wearing right now probably had more to do with how his eyes kept slipping down to check out Ann's extensive landscape.

"Hello, I'm Ann." Ann gave him one of those withering looks, you know the type. The "hey, my eyes are up here, not on my chest" sort of look. I

95

shook my head. If you're going to put fresh goods out on display, people are going to look, just saying. Honestly, I was amazed that the darn things had stayed put, what with all the jogging and zombie killing we'd been doing.

Jason cleared his throat and mumbled something close to a greeting then shifted his eyes away, gratefully settling on KL before asking, "Where'd you get her? The kid, I mean."

This time he did blush hard enough to see past his usual pink exterior.

"Under a table," KL smirked at him. She stepped out into a hall and looked around. "What is this place and how did you find it?"

"When I was unloading everything for the booth earlier I was talking to a janitor and he was just making conversation. He told me about these floors and where the elevator was," Jason explained. "He was pissed because only management is allowed up on the third floor and the A/C was out downstairs, but they wouldn't let them come up and use their breakroom."

KL nodded. "That figures, standard corporate crap."

Now that he mentioned it, it was patently obvious that this floor was a cut above the rest. The carpeting was clean and looked recently replaced, and the chairs were comfortable looking and heavily padded. The semi-industrial bright white walls were gone, too...replaced by a much more sedate cream color that didn't hurt my eyes. I had a feeling we just found the administrative offices, and that meant computers. My heart sped up. Computers meant internet access—if they weren't all locked down with passwords.

"Let's take this away from the elevator. Jason, do you have somewhere safe where we can regroup?"

"This whole floor is safe," he said, leading us toward a set of offices. We headed straight for the largest office. It was a huge affair with full length dark blue curtains lining the back wall and a couple of couches on either side.

None of that mattered. The minute I cleared the door, I saw what I wanted. There was a computer screen sitting at the edge of the executive desk facing us. Before I managed to make it two steps inside, my phone went insane, vibrating and pinging like crazy, with what seemed like a million notifications, tweets and messages all coming in at the same time.

"What the hell?" I fumbled in my pocket for the phone right as everyone else's cell phones started to go off.

"Give it to me," KL snatched it out of my hand. She had left hers in the truck. I barely noticed, there was something else I needed to see. While everyone pulled out their phones and waited for the cacophony of modern noise to end, I grabbed the thick blue curtains and closed my eyes for a moment before pulling them apart. It was just as I thought. The back wall was clear glass and overlooked the entire front half of the convention center. Stylized dolphin sculptures that had floated high above our heads from the main floor, now swam suspended from heavy line at eye level, but they didn't block the view to the city around us. "Holy crap, we're screwed," I whispered.

"Oh, my God...it's happening everywhere," Lauren gasped. She and Paul were huddled around her phone, watching a news video.

I turned and looked at the rest of the group, all hunched over tiny screens while they thumbed furiously through their messages. If it wasn't so sad, it would be funny. "Guys?"

No one answered me, they were too busy on their phones. For some reason, that made me angry. This time I raised my voice. "Guys!"

They all looked up at me.

I pointed a thumb over my shoulder. "You don't need your phones. It's all right there."

In all its glorious detail, the clear glass panes framed out the destruction of a city. We all lined up and watched, our phones forgotten. KL reached out and placed her palm on the glass. Was she trying to touch the carnage? The glass was a warm, sterile barrier that protected us from the smell and noise of what we were watching, much like watching TV with the sound off. It didn't stop me from imagining what it was like out there. Multiple plumes of smoke rose up in the air, some bigger and some smaller, and some being fed by live fires that burned without mercy through whole neighborhoods. Cars littered the road beneath us, some overturned and others wrecked up against each other like an impromptu urban demolition derby.

"What do you think caused this?" I asked no one in particular. My voice was faint and I felt like I could barely breathe.

"Maybe that weird ass cloud I mentioned this morning," KL said, earning points for managing to not sound sarcastic.

"Where's the police? Hell, where's the military? Somebody other than us has to still be alive," Brandon muttered.

"I can't see anything moving down there, but that doesn't mean anything, does it?" Paul said, reminding us that just because someone was moving, it didn't mean they were still in the land of the living.

A low rumble started to shake the windows. KL snatched her hand away from the glass and frowned when the rumble grew louder, then yelled. "Scatter."

We ducked and twisted away from the exposed location, pressing our bodies against the wall. A military helicopter swooped by, one of those new fancy ones that went wicked fast, then swerved away and kept moving out towards the water. We all chuckled at our overreaction and straightened up.

"Well, that's good news. All we have to do is wait for someone to find us," Brandon said, grinning in relief. "The military will know what to..."

He never got to finish his sentence.

"Fuck!" We all dived to the floor when an earth shaking explosion rocked the ground near us. "They're bombing the damn zombies!"

"Close the curtains, now!" I growled, then did it myself when no one moved.

"Why are you closing the curtains?" Brandon whined, "How will they find us if they can't see us?"

"If they see us, do you think they're going to check if we're alive? Or, do you think they're going to assume we're one of those things down there and shoot first, and ask questions later?" I asked. The city was burning, and now I knew why.

"So, what do we do then? Ride it out here, or what?"

I was leaning towards "or what", but I needed time to think. "We need more information. Right now everyone is freaking out. Overreacting. It could be more dangerous out there than in here, but eventually they will find us."

I didn't want to say what else I was thinking. The Con was full of zombies, not just hundreds, but probably thousands of them all trapped in here. There was no way a good commander would risk his troops going into a place like this. They would level the place and to hell with any survivors.

"I'm on it," KL said. She was furiously typing something on my phone.

"What are you doing?" I had to ask.

"Trying to get ahold of our friends," she answered.

"Good idea," I said, then headed for the computer. It wasn't until I sat down in the cushy leather chair that I realized just how tired my legs were. I wasn't the only one. Lauren and Paul had taken over one of the couches and Brandon had stretched out on the other one, plopping his combat boots on the pristine fabric like he was back in his living room. KL was leaning against the desk next to me and Bobby stood guard at the door. It was no use telling him to relax, he wouldn't do it unless someone gave him a direct order, and even then I wasn't sure if he would stand down. Jason was with him, chatting gaily in what was a decidedly one sided conversation. If I didn't know better, he was having the time of his life. He practically vibrated with excitement.

A couple of key hits later and the screen was no longer black, but it sure wasn't giving up its secrets either. The password request page stared back at me in blank smugness. There was no way I would ever guess what the heck it was and computer hacking wasn't in my skillset. Growling, I tossed the keyboard down in disgust and contemplated clearing the desktop of its contents. That's how frustrated I was.

"Okay, what do we know? Any news worth actually sharing?" I asked Paul and Lauren.

"Just videos showing the same thing we saw. Everyone going still then total havoc when they woke up or whatever," Lauren answered.

"There is no official news that I have been able to find," Jason said. "Just people talking about all of the accidents and asking everyone to stay indoors until the government can give them a clearer picture of what's going on. One news channel is claiming it's just rioters going out and looting, overturning cars, starting fires, stuff like that. The fringe channels are claiming it's a takeover by a hostile country, or a hostile attack on the USA by our own government, they can't decide. The religious folk are claiming it's either Armageddon, or the Rapture and are claiming demons are running through the streets to claim all the sinners. Pick your brand of aluminum foil with any of those types."

"As far as I can tell, the only thing that everyone agrees on is that whatever this is, a whole lot of people have been affected. People just froze doing whatever they were doing, with no warning," Paul continued.

That meant driving, flying, everything. Holy shit. No wonder everything was such a clusterfuck.

"So, why are we still getting phone access and internet?" Ann asked. "We still have electricity and I'm going to assume running water."

"A lot of that stuff is computerized. Unless there's damage to something mechanical it should keep running until someone turns it off." I wasn't sure about that, but it was the only suggestion I could think of.

"Do you think this is some sort of experiment?" Paul asked.

"I have no idea. I mean, what would be the point?" I asked.

"They are the Soulless," Carol Ann popped up with. Her voice was so somber, and she uttered it with such belief in that childish voice that it creeped me out. I saw Lauren shudder and look away, so it wasn't just me.

"Sorry. She slipped away from me," Ann said.

I just waved away the apology.

"So what are we going to do? We can't stay here forever," Lauren asked.

Carol Ann escaped from Ann again and ran up to KL.

"Revenant Chaser? Where is my mom?" she asked, tugging at my wife's long coat. She looked frightened, which meant she knew this wasn't a game anymore. This was majorly going to suck. What were we going to tell a little girl? My wife was not known for being a kid person. Sure, she had a soft spot for them and baby animals, but she had a habit of just telling things like they were. How do you tell a little girl that their momma was either dead, or a flesh eating zombie wandering around downstairs looking for people snacks?

"I don't know, Carol Ann," she answered, kneeling down to be closer to the little girl's height. "Why don't you tell me where you saw her last?"

"We were watching the Spider-Men fighting, and she wanted to keep going and I wanted to stay. Then she stopped moving and wouldn't talk to me and I thought she was mad at me and I started crying and ran back to our booth. I got lost and then I got scared because no one would talk to me, so I hid under the table." Tears bubbled up in the corner of her eyes and her chin quivered. "Revenant Chaser, did the Soulless get my mommy and brother?"

"You don't have to call her Revenant Chaser, kid. It's just an act," Brandon spat out with unnecessary sarcasm.

"Brandon, stop being a dick," I snapped. My wife had saved his life today and he still couldn't tone down the attitude. This was a whole new side of him and I was really getting over it.

"I don't know, kid. But Brandon is right about one thing. These aren't revenants like in the comic book, and I'm no hero." KL stood up and shot me a pleading look. She actually looked physically sick.

Thankfully, Ann stepped in and took the little girl's hand. "I'll try to keep her out of your all's hair. Come on sweetie, let's find something for you to eat, you'll feel better."

"No!" Carol Ann yelled and pulled her hand away. She turned on KL and me and then pointed straight at her. "They are revenants, can't you see? They are the Soulless, and they're angry because we have something they don't anymore."

What the hell? KL stared at me and I just shrugged and shook my head. "I have no idea."

Bobby watched the two of them walk out into the hallway, then turned to face the rest of the group. "That wasn't creepy at all."

Leave it to the man of few words to choose the words we were all thinking.

"Yeah, not creepy at all." I shook myself like a dog to get rid of the heebie-jeebies dancing on my spine and turned back to Jason. Now that Ann mentioned it, no one had eaten since early morning and zombie killing was hard work. A meal wouldn't be a bad idea. "Are there any snacks around?"

"Yeah, there's a fridge down the hall in the breakroom."

"Alright, let's go see what it has," I said. "We need to eat, no matter what's decided."

It wasn't necessary to remind them that whatever we found might become a last meal, but I refused to accept that this situation was going to become our apocalyptic green mile.

KL

I walked into the breakroom last only to encounter a scene right out of a bad caveman movie. The guys were crowded around the refrigerator, backs hunched over like troglodytes as they disemboweled the rectangular box as gleefully as a pack of jackal's dismembering a gazelle. All we needed was a soundtrack full of grunts and hooting and the scene would be complete.

"Animals," Roxy muttered when she caught sight of them, just in time for Paul to rear up and spin away with a flat box in hand.

He raised it high above him like a trophy and crowed, "Pizza! Thank you, God." Then headed for the microwave.

"No. No microwave." Lauren took the box away from him and added it to the rest of the spoils. A large, round table took up a good bit of real estate in the middle of the floor, with about a dozen chairs strewn about.

"Aww. Why not?" Paul asked. Jason and Brandon were right behind him, their arms full of miscellaneous Tupperware, Chinese food containers and lunch bags. They both echoed his disappointment, but were also promptly relieved of their booty by Lauren and Ann.

"Because," Lauren said, rolling her eyes at the men like it should be patently obvious. "We don't know who is out there still, let alone if it might attract those things downstairs. Do you really want to send, let's see..." she opened up the pizza box. "The delicious smell of hot cheese and pepperoni through the air vents?"

I swear I could hear them salivating. It was probably mean of Lauren to tease them like that, but we were all in the same boat. It was cold food or no food, because I wasn't going to be zombie bait so someone could burn their tongue on greasy cheese.

"Don't pout, boys. I'm sure you've eaten plenty of cold pizza over the years. Don't get all fancy on us now," I said, picking up one of the Chinese food containers and popping it open before promptly shutting it. It was too soon after gutting a zombie to even look at the congealed mass of thick noodles and sliced pork without wanting to throw up.

"Oh, ick. I'm not even sure a microwave would fix that," Ann said, pulling apart limp bread and even limper lettuce to reveal the insides of a half-eaten sub sandwich that had seen better days. Unless the meat was supposed to be that particular shade of gray, I wasn't going anywhere near that. Even the cheese had turned pale and bloated reminding me more of whale blubber than something that was supposed to be a milk product that was good for you and chock full of calcium.

Yeah, right. I was beginning to wonder about the sort of people this place employed.

The refrigerator was practically a living biology experiment, with all sorts of interesting secondary life forms growing in there. The freezer was better, mostly because it was full of flat boxes boldly labeled with names in black marker, but unless someone wanted to chomp down on some frozen burritos our newly enacted no microwave rule crossed that option out.

"Toss it. I'm sure we can find enough food that's still good for everyone to share," Roxy said, emphasizing the word share. She cleared her throat, then crossed her arms when words alone didn't quite have the desired effect. Cold blue eyes turned even colder and even I shivered a little bit. Roxy wasn't a tall woman, but she had a way about her that said don't fuck with me. She also outweighed each of the men standing there, except for Jason, and most of it was earned in the gym. I'm not sure who would win if it ever became a one on one fight, but that would never happen, not with me there. We were a team, and we didn't fight fair.

I guess that would make the list as Rule Number 5: Honor and the concept of fighting a fair fight is fine and great, unless it's going to get you killed. Real life isn't laid out on a chessboard battlefield, its freaking guerrilla warfare.

Greedy hands rapidly removed themselves from the pizza slices they had already claimed.

Jason had the good graces to blush and Paul mumbled an apology. But Brandon, bless his heart...he had already taken a bite of his slice and he looked straight at us and deliberately took another bite and chewed on it through a completely unabashed grin. He shrugged and plunked down on a seat next to the sink, pulled up another chair to put his boots up on and proceeded to ignore everyone else.

"What's his problem?" Jason asked around a mouthful of sandwich.

I could smell the tuna fish, along with a healthy helping of onions, but otherwise it looked safe. Ann had gone through all the food and had made herself the impromptu lunch lady, handing out sandwiches and leftovers to everyone after making sure Carol Ann got something she would actually eat. She was surprisingly complacent about eating a cold lunch, which was more than I could say about the guys.

"Hell if I know. He's been a right pain since all of this started," I said, rubbing my forehead against an impending headache. "But I really am not prepared to play babysitter, especially not for the entire zombie apocalypse."

"He'll get himself straightened out. It might just take a little time," Jason said, showing more confidence in his friend than I had at the moment.

"I hope so. It's not like you can plan for something like this. Well, you can, but that doesn't mean a damn thing once shit gets real," I said, fully understanding the irony of what I was saying. Playacting was one thing, but this was the real deal. So far, Brandon wasn't passing his trial by fire very well.

Roxy used to tell me stories about soldiers who were all gung ho about the military until they were deployed. You just never know who's going to step up and do what's needed and who was going to turn into a complete basket case...and that's with proper training. The most training Brandon had was a penchant for watching Full Metal Jacket at least once a week and following it up with a chaser of Apocalypse Now.

Roxy wandered over and handed me a Tupperware and a can of Coke.

"Look what I found. I had to trade it for a candy bar but it was worth it."

"Oh, yeah," I grinned and gave my wife a quick peck on the cheek before popping the tab. It was only after I had downed half the can that I stopped and gave her a sheepish look. "Sorry about the candy bar."

"That's okay," she lowered her voice a bit. "Someone was holding one of those fundraisers for a buck a bar. No one liked dark chocolate, so I called dibs on the whole lot." She winked, then noticed I hadn't bothered with my sandwich yet. "I hope you don't mind peanut butter and jelly. I had saved it for

Carol Ann, but she didn't want it. Weird, huh? A kid that doesn't like PB & J?"

I didn't mind, but I was still peeved about Brandon and that meant I was only half listening to what Roxy was saying. I think I was about half way through my sandwich and wishing she had found two cokes instead of one when Roxy piped up again.

"I swear that man could come in last during a circle jerk and claim he won," she said, raising an eyebrow at me before purposefully eyeing Brandon.

Jason whistled, trying not to smile but failing. "Damn, that's harsh."

That did the trick. Despite myself I broke out laughing, which only made Brandon frown at us, which then made me laugh even harder. She knew me too well. That was something I appreciated every day of my life, and even more so after I started to choke on sticky peanut butter and bread that decided to stick to the back of my throat and refused to go down any farther. Mostly because she dug out another can of Coke and handed it to me without a single word.

"Maybe, but he's not winning anybody over acting like that," Roxy said, leveling a troubled look in Brandon's direction. She looked like she was going to say more, but instead she surprised us both by changing subjects completely. That probably had more to do with Jason than me. She knew Jason was close to Brandon, in that male bonding buddy-buddy way that the estrogen laden could never understand or overcome...no matter how badass they were. "But that's not what I came over here to talk about. You were spying on us with the security system cameras in order to guide us up here, right?"

"Yeah?" Jason cocked his head to the side curiously. I'm sure his eyebrows climbed higher on his forehead, but they were so pale it was hard to tell. Damn gingers.

"We need to see that room."

Roxy

We were all back in what I assumed was the corporate manager's office, since it was decked out with the best furniture. It was also the biggest office and size matters in the corporate world. Somehow, I was back behind the big desk and everyone was looking at me expectantly. Well, almost everyone.

"Okay, everyone's fed and we've had a bit of a rest, so now it's decision time," I started, leaning back into the leather cushions behind my back. KL stood next to me, her hand resting on the chair above my shoulder. For all intents and purposes she just seemed to be hanging out there and relaxing, but it felt like she was playing bodyguard to my mafia boss laying it all on the line. "Look here, see...this is how it's gonna be." Except none of us were wearing suits and fedora's and the enemy wasn't another gang on the other side of town trying to push into our territory. Nope, these were zombies we were dealing with, and not the fun ones that had rhythm and danced in the street, flash mob style.

"Jason showed us the security cameras. From what I can see, we're safe here, but only if they don't notice us. That means we're essentially treed up here even if the hounds haven't caught our scent."

"What about the police or the military? Has anyone tried to contact anyone?" Paul asked.

KL fielded that answer. "The lines keep coming up circuit busy and even social media has gone dark. I think the military has their hands full, too full to worry about a half-dozen stragglers."

That was the scariest part. Everyone, and I do mean everyone from toddlers to retirees, seemed plastered to their phone these days. People would pull out their phones before they'd think to pull a victim from a burning building and upload it to the internet so they could show all their friends. The elusive viral video had become something desirable, a ribbon of honor in a world rapidly losing its humanity to soundbites and numbers of shares.

"You couldn't find any other survivors?" Brandon asked, throwing his question out like a challenge.

"Not inside the convention center. We scanned every area that had cameras and didn't see anybody else that looked alive. Anybody that didn't make it out in those first few minutes, more than likely didn't make it out at all. We're the only ones left," I said, trying to ignore the images I couldn't erase plastered on the inside of my eyeballs. There was something doubly disturbing about zombies dressed as superhero's munching on shit sausage while tearing open some poor overweight geek like a bread bowl at the local diner. That hurt, because I really liked Kielbasa, and I wasn't sure if I could ever look at it the same way again.

In retrospect, I had to ask myself if we should have done the same, then I wondered how many of the less savory types never made it home. They had been so intent on looting they were weighed down by boxes of collectibles that were heavy enough to slow a pack animal. I smirked. How ironic it was, to die carting out something that instantly went from rare and valuable, to something worth less than toilet paper or firewood. A zombie apocalypse changes everything.

"Maybe they're hiding somewhere, like us," Brandon insisted, popping up from his chair to lean on the desk in front of us. Maybe he was trying to loom, or at least look a little bit threatening, but all he did was offend me with his breath.

"Please sit back down, Brandon," I said in my calmest voice while trying to breathe through my mouth. An ear twitching, nails on chalkboard noise behind me made me shudder. KL was digging her fingers into the padded leather.

I ignored the implication that we hadn't looked long or hard enough, but KL couldn't. "That's true. There might be one or two. But we're not going to spend the next two days trying to find them. The only reason we're still here and didn't make it to our vehicles is because we stuck around to look for Tommy. Everyone else cut and run."

"Are you saying we shouldn't have gone looking for him? That we should have just took off like everyone else?" Brandon asked. Bobby's face went cold, then crumpled. He had been doing so well, too.

Brandon didn't sit down. His jaw jutted out like a fighter daring someone to take a swing at him, a huge temptation right now. The man just made me tired, he really did.

I jumped out of my chair hard enough for it to spin away. KL kept it from slamming into the glass behind me, then stepped aside with a knowing grin. She knew what was coming and evidently wanted a good view of the show.

"Way to go, Brandon. Why not just remind Bobby and the rest of us that one of us is still down there?" I hissed. Tommy had been frozen, which meant the next time we ran into him he would be one of those things, all hungry and not human. I prayed that wouldn't happen. It was one thing taking out a stranger, but quite another to take a blade to a friend, even if he was trying to eat you.

"And that's exactly why we need to stay put and wait for help to come to us!" he yelled, eyes flashing fearfully. His outburst had gotten the rest of the group's attention. Everyone was standing, and no one looked happy. Ann took Carol Ann's hand and murmured something about finding some crayons and slinked out the door with a worried expression on her face and a plastic smile for the kid.

"I'm only going to say this one more time, Brandon." Cold fury froze my heart and made every word come out with careful precision. "Sit. Down."

He sat. He even managed to shut up even though it looked like it was causing him physical pain. His expression had gone from merely constipated to gas cramps, but I didn't care. As long as he kept his little ball of negativity reined in, he could just sit there and stew.

A deep breath in and out and I was much calmer. We all found our seats again and got down to business.

"We've got two ways out of here, the back fire stair well and the elevator." Jason leaned forward in his seat and pointed down the hall. Now that we were making plans everyone seemed eager to get going. They were afraid, it was easy to see that in their eyes and how nervously they shifted in their seats, but they were putting a brave face on and doing all anyone could do in a situation like this— plan like hell and hope it all works out. They kept glancing at each other, then looking away guiltily. Their thoughts were plain to anyone paying attention to them. Everyone was wondering who would make it out and who wouldn't.

"We can't use the elevator, at least not down to the first floor. There's a mess there, and it's attracted every zombie in smelling distance," KL said. My wife had unslung her bow and spent a few minutes examining it while she silently listened before speaking up. It wasn't her most expensive bow, but it was her favorite since she had made it specifically for her draw and weight. It was also pretty damn accurate.

"Okay, so that's out. What about the escalators?" I asked. The fire stairs exited near the elevators so that meant they were out, too. "I know we sealed the doors to the main convention room, so that means any zombies have to find the path through the food courts, right?"

The building's design helped quite a bit. The food courts had long, thin access isles to keep people from slipping into the show without paying, as well as rope guides to keep them in neat little docile lines. The food court would act like a cattle chute, only allowing a few out at a time and only if they found the opening. The zombies from earlier had worked in there so they didn't need to find the place, just escape from it.

"The down escalators are safe going from the second to the first floor but the up escalators on either side are a problem. The second floor is pretty much a deck with an overlook and smaller exhibit rooms beneath us. Most of them were empty anyway so that helps. Right now there's not much reason for any of them to go up the escalator but if they see us it could get ugly."

Bobby raised his hand, just like a little kid in school waiting for the teacher to notice him. He looked excited. "I have something that might help with the escalators. It should give us a few more minutes and maybe distract the zombies."

"Good. Does anybody else have any ideas?" I asked, looking around the room.

"Weapons." I turned to look at KL. She had removed one of the fake arrows from her quiver and was twirling it around in her hand. "We need more weapons."

She tossed the arrow up into the air and caught it mid shaft, then grinned. "They wouldn't let me in with any real arrows, but these are hardwood. I can easily sharpen them."

"I suggest we split up and start hunting for anything that can be used as a weapon. Look for toolboxes, knives, screwdrivers, anything that can be used to take out a zombie."

"Right. Nothing they've done is anything like we've seen in the movies or books, other than trying to kill us. I don't know if that body shot KL took at the elevator killed that one or if the others did it tearing him up," I paused and let that sink in. "This is good news though, we know they will attack each other once they're injured. Maybe because they are all so fresh they can't tell the dead from the living, I don't know. We do know the tried and true headshot does work, so anything that will poke a hole in someone's brainbox should be everyone's focus."

"I think we should..." Brandon finally decided to stop sulking and participate again.

"Yes?"

"I don't think we should do this. There's what? A hundred? A thousand zombies down there? And what about outside? The parking lot could be crawling with those things." He crossed his arms and stood there glaring at me.

The sad thing was, all of those points were completely valid, and ones that had been on my mind the whole time, but sitting here was going to do nothing but get us all killed.

"Yeah? You don't think we haven't thought about that? We all know that out there is an unknown, but staying here? That's suicide. What about food? Water? Huh? How many days do you think we can survive up here, hiding like mice in a bare cupboard? It's going to be dark in a few hours and what then? We won't have the option of leaving...we won't be able to navigate the streets the way they are now. If we don't go now, we may never get a chance to." I was so mad I was talking with my hands, counting off each point with my fingers and wishing I could just jam them in his throat.

"Well, I'm not going. I think what you're planning is suicide. We should figure out a way to make a signal so someone could find us."

"Oh?" I asked, facing him chest to chest. He was a few inches taller than me but I was hopping mad and didn't care. Sarcasm had joined the fray and was begging to be let into the ring. "How? You want to set the place on fire and send smoke signals, hmm?"

"I should have never let you join, you and your Revenant Chaser with all your comic book groupies," he spat, his face turning beet red. "This is my group, not yours. You can leave if you want to, but I'm not letting you take everyone with you."

"No, you were in charge of a fake group. That is it. This is real life now," I calmly told him. All the others had moved away from him...except for my wife. She had been calmly sharpening the wooden dowel arrows with Bobby's knife, but now she had her sword in hand. Her face was death.

"You need to shut up, now! Are you trying to broadcast our location to every zombie in the building?"

"You aren't my boss, I'm a grown ass man."

I'm not sure what he was going to say next, but a very sharp point just under the chin certainly did the trick to stop his nonsense. He rolled his eyes, trying to see down his nose, but KL kept him on his tiptoes. "Be quiet or I will make sure you don't speak again. You are endangering all of us."

"Sweetie, you can't kill him in front of Carol Ann," Lauren spoke softly, touching KL's sleeve.

"Fine, but one more word and I am pushing him out the door," she grumbled, then plopped back down and started sharpening her arrows.

Brandon wiped at his neck like he was checking for spiders, then looked at his hand. When he didn't see any blood, his entire demeanor changed. He puffed up his chest like a peacock and straightened up as tall as he could make himself. He must have coaxed his balls out from whatever body cavity they had crawled into because he looked like he was ready to start arguing again. My wife just gave him a bored look and stood up with a freshly sharpened arrow in her hand, then calmly nocked an arrow.

"Now, do you have something constructive to say?" she asked him, drawing the bow and aiming it straight at his left eye.

Wise man kept his mouth shut.

"We could just put him in a corner and gag him," Paul suggested. It looked like he didn't trust Brandon to remain quiet, either. Hell, he had already proven himself a coward and a thief, but I still had to think about it.

I imagined him sitting in a corner like a naughty boy being put in time out until he learned to play nice with everyone else. That was such a lovely, gratifying image...and perhaps he would learn something before the shit hit the fan and we needed him. I wouldn't leave him like that, exposed and vulnerable to those things downstairs, but he didn't know that, did he?

Gratified that the rest of the group was backing me up, I nodded in agreement, then was surprised when it was Bobby who took him to the corner and stuffed a rag in his mouth. I hadn't expected that.

Jason was frowning. He had remained Switzerland through all the drama but now I had to know. "Are you okay with this?"

He shrugged, then gave me a flat look and an even flatter response, the type you give someone in charge when you don't like their decision but you'll stand by it. "I guess he had it coming."

"Okay, then," I said, trying to put more enthusiasm into it than I felt. "Let's find some weapons and get this show on the road."

"Looks like you are the leader now," KL said, smiling at me, then helped usher everyone out of the room.

I waited for everyone to leave before yawning. No one told me the Zombie Apocalypse was going to be so damn exhausting.

KL

Everyone scattered, intent on finding items for what had to be the strangest scavenger hunt in history. They were surprisingly effective, blowing through the floor with the destructive force of a small swarm of locusts while they tore through desks, storage bins and closets. Evidently, there was no going down with the ship here at The Con. Our little team of Zombie Hunters were proving to be enthusiastic and efficient thieves. I had no idea.

As soon as everyone else was busy hunting up possible weapons, I pulled Roxy off to the side. "I want to go check out the cameras again."

I had an idea brewing but I needed to get a closer look at the stair wells.

She looked at me funny, but didn't ask why I was being so sneaky about it. She just waited, not saying a thing until we were by ourselves. The door to the security room closed behind us and I locked it for a bit of privacy. Roxy cast a quick glance at the display screens then turned her back on them to look at me.

"Okay, what's up?"

"Are you doing okay?

"I could ask you the same," Roxy shrugged. "Why?"

"I know you aren't happy about having to take the leadership role."

"It is what it is," Roxy said.

She frowned but didn't fight me too hard when I put my arms around her. It didn't last long but it didn't need to. A hug was a hug and always appreciated, but when you're trying to keep your emotions in check, a hug could become the pulled stopper that let loose a good cryfest. That was not in our best interest right now. Right now we had to be hard, especially around the guys. Guys never understood why a woman cried and had a tendency to think it was a sign of weakness. It didn't matter that it was an erroneous assumption. Appearances were everything. Respect was everything. Respect and trust. We needed that to keep us all alive.

"That's enough, now," Roxy sniffed, then let me go after a quick peck on the cheek. "We've got things to do and no time to be mushy. We can relax when we get back home."

"Well, until then you have me to back you up and obviously Bobby is on our side. Lauren, Paul, and Ann? They already look to you for answers, so that just leaves Jason...and Brandon." I practically spit the last name out.

"You're worried about Jason?" she asked, focusing on that last pause all too quickly.

I considered that question for a few seconds before answering. "Well, he's known Brandon for a while, and we only just met him when we joined the

Zombie Response Team. I don't know how good of friends they are. He could be more loyal to Brandon than to us. I think if we had to choose between keeping both of them or letting them both go, I'd let Brandon walk. Jason's a strong fighter, but Brandon is going to get someone killed eventually."

Roxy looked at me, then chuckled. I think she was impressed. "Maybe you should be the leader," she suggested.

"Yeah, like that would work out well. I would have killed Brandon instead of just gagging him," I said, curling my lower lip against a bitter taste in my mouth. That still rankled me a bit, but I understood why Roxy and Lauren held me back. I didn't have to like it, but I understood it.

"I'm not so sure about that. You did pretty well back there."

"No, you have the training for it. I'm better as backup." I just couldn't get over that nagging sense that we were making a mistake. There are a few good rules from the movies you could live by. Never turn your back after knocking out the bad guy, they'll inevitably get up when your back is turned and kill your ass—and never let the coward live. They'll sell you out the first time they have a chance.

I wasn't joking about killing Brandon. It wasn't a moral dilemma for me. Roxy says that part of me is broken, but I enjoyed being able to make decisions out of practicality, not social expectations. It was Roxy's job to temper that with necessity. She was my moral compass, and in return, I was the one person she couldn't boss around. That's what made us such a good team in the first place. We balanced each other.

"So what are you thinking then? Cause I know you have a plan."

"The stairwells have cameras."

"What? I didn't know that."

"I saw them when Jason was scrolling through. We were obviously more focused on the main areas, but now I need a better look."

"What are you thinking?"

"They're a clear shot down without having to deal with the elevator and so far, the zombies haven't discovered them.

"That just might work," Roxy said, leaning over my shoulder.

"Yeah, the only problem is that," I said, pointing out the congregation of zombies that were still feasting on one of their own. There were more of them than I remembered and not much left of the ones we had dealt with, but more importantly, they were wall to wall along the hallway we'd have to take to get out.

"So, the first floor is going to be a problem. How does it look near the escalators?"

The system was unfamiliar but after a few tries I figured out how to work the keyboard and mouse and pick out specific areas to zoom in on. Roxy's eyes were glued on the scene at the elevator.

"That is so weird...and gross. I know we can't go by the movies, but why are they eating each other?" she asked.

"I really don't know. I think you're explanation might be best. Maybe they're so fresh they can't tell the difference between the living and the dead. But really, who the fuck knows," I said, then cocked my head as a promising idea started to form. If they weren't following the old rules, then neither should I. Besides, making my own was so much more fun.

I guess that would be Zombie Hunting Rule Number 6: Not everything you learned in the movies can be trusted. If something doesn't work, throw it out the window and keep experimenting.

Roxy interrupted my thoughts with a new one. She had found a pencil and was twirling it around between her fingertips. "I'm wondering about something Carol Ann said. She keeps calling those things the soulless."

"Okay? It's obvious she's a fan of the Revenant Chaser. These things aren't revenants like in our comic book, but they're close enough to confuse a little girl."

"Yeah, I don't really know what I am getting at. It's like a half-thought stuck in my head," she shook her head, then smiled apologetically. "It's probably silly."

"I understand, babe," I said, then leaned forward to stop Roxy from getting up. All this talk about Carol Ann gave me an idea. "Hey, before we leave, do you think this was recording the whole time?"

"I have no idea. Why?"

"I was just thinking maybe we could locate where Carol Ann had been. See if her mom is among the living or formerly frozen."

"So we know what she looks like in case we run into her on the way out," Roxy said, her voice flat and emotionless.

Her response made it pretty obvious that she didn't think the woman was alive any more than I did. Which meant the next time we met, she wouldn't be worried about why we kidnapped her child, she'd be in the mood for lunch...and Carol Ann didn't need to see that.

"Yeah, pretty much."

Roxy took over and started fiddling with the computers. After a few minutes of cursing and fighting with the system, she figured it out. The screens went fuzzy and the date stamp in the corner started rolling backward. She grinned at me in triumph and pointed at the monitor. "There she is."

"Huh. Can you run it forward in real time now?" I asked, leaning in to get a closer look. Out of everything we'd seen today this was the weirdest by far.

"Yeah, I think so. Here, I got it now." She hit a few more buttons and the video started moving again. "What the hell?"

Her mouth dropped open and she glanced over at me as if to verify we were seeing the same thing before her eyes shot straight back to the grainy screen.

Carol Ann was skipping through the mass of bodies. None of them were attacking her or paying any attention to her. Some of them were moving, still a little sluggishly, but she just wove in and out of them without a care. She even touched one or two of them in a tagging motion before continuing on. All she needed was a red cloak and she was the very picture of another little girl skipping through an entirely different kind of a dangerous forest so she could visit her grandmother. Only this time, she was skipping past a forest of wolves who we knew were hungry, but none of them seemed interested in this particular morsel. It was uncanny and more than a little unsettling to watch.

She made it through the doors and into the registration area where we had found her, then she paused and looked up...straight at the camera, and waved gaily, before crawling under the table. The video sputtered and spit into badly pixelated fuzz then cleared up, just as we appeared in the screen to find and rescue her.

Where was the scared little girl?

"Can you go back any farther?" I asked my wife. We still hadn't seen Carol Ann's mother.

She fiddled with the controls some more, then the screen went blank. "Dammit, I can't get it to do anything else." Roxy slapped her palm down on the table hard enough to make the mouse jump, then looked up at me with a hopeful expression on her face. "Maybe it's on a loop and can only save for so many hours at a time?"

That explanation was as good as any, but it didn't satisfy the creeped out, crawling up my back sensation that would normally have me stripping to find a tick, spider, or god forbid, a praying mantis. I blew out my breath and tried not to squirm.

"Um, Roxy? What the hell is going on here?" I was starting to feel like we had woke up in some strange alternate universe inside of one of our own comic books, requisite creepy kid included.

"I hate to keep sounding like a broken record, but I have no idea. All we can do right now is concentrate on the matter at hand and get out of here."

She was right. We needed to stay focused on the immediate future. I know neither one of us would forget what we had just seen though. This just wasn't the time to dwell on it.

"I agree. Let's go see how the others have done finding weapons. I've seen enough here to know what we need to do to get out of here, and I think this place is going to help us," I said, eyeing the pile of CD's stacked on the corner of the desk.

"Just out of curiosity, what are you thinking?" Roxy asked, unlocking the door and waving me through. "You know, since I'm supposed to be in charge and all that, it might be nice if I'm on the same sheet of music."

"Funny you should say that," I said, then smiled. My idea could go really wrong or really right, but at least it would be interesting. Besides, I had been denied a soundtrack this whole time, and one must have just the right music to accompany the badassery that was about to ensue.

Roxy

Well, we had a plan. It was a sucky plan full of holes big enough to drive a Mack truck through, but we had to do something. We only had a few hours to go before the sun was going to set, and none of us wanted to still be here when that happened. Well except for Brandon, and he didn't count right now.

There was a reason humans had an instinctive fear of the dark, and no matter how technical or advanced society had become, we were all still reduced to hiding in a cave and hoping fire would keep the monsters at bay until morning came. An old sergeant I used to know, a crusty old sucker that had survived Vietnam with a tear gas induced voice that reminded me of gravel scraping against concrete, liked to remind me there weren't any atheists in a foxhole.

I wasn't too sure about that, not when I watched his eye's glaze over with hellish memories that didn't match the wolfish grin that exposed tobacco stained teeth. Sometimes it's not faith I would see tempering the fear in the eyes of those soldiers, it was the dark glittering stare of our ancestors. They knew death waited for them with

137

every hunt, and that knowledge kept them humble. Their hearts weren't filled with the irrational hubris of modern man who wrote laws for the world and self-proclaimed themselves the favorite of whatever Gods they followed.

We weren't the top of the food chain, never were and certainly we weren't now, not without buildings to keep us warm, weapons to uneven the playing field, and technology to cater to our every whim. All it takes to put us back in that cave, cowering around the glow of a campfire and clutching sharpened sticks while we tried not to piss ourselves is the realization that we were now the one's being hunted.

"Hey, your face will freeze like that if you aren't careful."

I jumped, and would have fallen out my seat if KL hadn't kept the chair from spinning away from me. The nightstick fell off the table and clattered to the floor and we both bent over at the same time to pick it up.

"Jeez, babe. You trying to give me a concussion or something?" KL asked, straightening up with the stick in one hand and rubbing her forehead with the other. I had barely registered the dull thud as a sound, but I was the one with a thick skull.

"Would that keep you from going?" I asked, placing the nightstick back down on the table, a little farther away from me this time.

"You know I have to go. No one else knows how to shoot the bow, and Jason can't be trusted," she said, glancing over at the bottle of whiskey I had confiscated.

It was opened and almost half empty, thanks to Jason bogarting his little find. I leaned forward and twisted the card hanging around the neck by a colorful bow so I could read it. "Congratulations on surviving 20 years, enjoy your retirement!"

"Do you think he's going to?" I asked.

"Going to what?"

"Enjoy his retirement." It was a pretty pricey bottle of booze and the poor man never had a chance to drink it. That bites, no pun intended.

I tore off the card and crumpled it in my hand. The sharp edge of the thick card stock bit into my palm so I gripped it even tighter, daring it to hurt me before I turned the offensive paper into a useless ball of nothing.

"Dark thoughts," KL said, then gave me a sharp look. "Should I know something? Do you have a bad feeling about this?"

Instead of answering her, I looked up at the security screens. Each rectangle contained a grainy gray image of the different areas of the convention center and almost every single one of them showed movement. If you unfocused your eyes, you could almost pretend you were looking at the boring inner workings of a worm farm, almost...until you realized you were watching humanity feeding upon itself. I couldn't do that. I couldn't just lose focus and pretend this wasn't real. This wasn't something I could just un-see, not when we were preparing to get up close and personal again with all the nastiness. I looked over at my wife and shook my head. Of course I had a bad feeling about all of this. "I've been wondering. This is a pretty high-tech setup. Why is this place wired like freaking Fort Knox?"

"Well, they do gun shows here sometimes. They probably don't want anyone stealing guns or selling them without paperwork."

She was probably right. The country was too damned paranoid, especially in the last few years since the fundamentals went all "end of times" on us and tried to take over. "Jason said no one was home when he got up here. I guess we rate second fiddle as a security risk, eh? No one worries about the Justice League marching on Washington or blowing up a women's clinic."

She waved her hand dismissively and grinned back at me. "Whoever was manning this place probably knew what was going on before any of us did. I'm betting he bailed for home way before the shit hit the fan for real."

"Nice of him to warn us," I growled.

KL laughed aloud, then playfully backed away when I turned a baleful glare her way. "Sure, babe...I can just hear him announcing a zombie apocalypse over the loudspeaker."

"Yup...and then asking everyone to leave in an orderly fashion through the appropriate exits?" I suggested, snickering at the visual image.

We laughed together then KL sobered up. "Too bad no such option was left for us. I guess we should get to this, huh? We're all ready, are you?"

"Yeah. I still don't like it, but I'm ready."

"I know you don't like sitting this one out, but we won't be apart, not really." She waved at the screens. "You can see me and everything going on around us. That means you can warn us way before anything gets too close. You can't do that if you're out there with us."

"I know, I know."

KL pulled me out of the chair and pulled me close. "Hey, I'm not going to do anything stupid. Not this time. You yell run, and I'll run," she said softly, then kissed me. "I promise. We'll be back before you know it, then you better be ready to run for real because we're about to kick the hornets' nest. For better or worse, babe, we're going for the ultimate jailbreak here."

I was set up in the security room, but that didn't mean I was going to just let her go. We walked back to the emergency stairwell together, not really talking, but making sure we touched. KL kept checking her gear, reaching behind her to check her arrow placement then running her hand back to the sword hilt at her hip.

Bobby and Paul were waiting for us. Bobby was practically vibrating with excitement, while Paul was being fussed at by Lauren. Watching the two of them behaving the same way I felt helped me feel better about being such a worry wart. "Do you guys have everything you need?"

Bobby held up his prize. He tossed the screwdriver so it spun above his head, then neatly snatched it out of the air and brandished it like a knife. "I'm good. Just get us to the escalators."

"Great. Just don't lose the damn thing in someone's skull. Use your knife. Save the screwdriver for the escalator," I said, trying not to think about what his little trick was going to do if it worked the way we hoped.

"What about you, Paul?" He had a sort of mop hybrid in his hand, replete with some kind of Lucite trophy duct taped to the end. It looked heavy and awkward but perfectly capable of denting a skull or two. He had also found a pretty wicked looking letter opener that wouldn't cut butter but looked like a pretty good stabbing weapon.

"I'm good."

"Okay." I took a deep breath and assumed my practical, this is the way it is voice. "So from what I can see, the second floor is pretty clear, but there aren't any cameras inside the smaller rooms so I can't say that for sure. Don't get yourself trapped between those rooms and the escalators. I'll be on the cameras and will break through if I see anything. Like KL said, if I yell run...run. Don't hesitate and don't break ranks. We'll secure the doors behind you and regroup back here on the third floor. If everything works the way we expect it too, we'll be on the move soon enough. Once we've attracted enough of the zombies to the front hall, we'll head out the back and get to our vehicles."

Before they filed out, I grabbed KL's sleeve. "Be safe," I whispered, then caught Paul's attention. I didn't ask him to watch out for her, but he nodded as if he understood what I was thinking.

The door closed behind them with a solid snick and they were on their way. I had to fight the urge to call them back before it was too late. A few seconds later, the door reopened and Lauren peeked her head out.

"Roxy?" Lauren asked, her voice sounded rough and I realized she was even more scared than I was.

"You shouldn't be up here." I know I sounded brusque, but I was pretty much running on empty when it came to social niceties. It was Lauren's job to keep the stairwell door secured while they were gone, but more importantly, she needed to get that door open quick when they came back. Until now, we hadn't had to worry about the stairwell. The first thing Jason had done when he secured the third floor was to kick blocks beneath the doors on each floor. As long as there wasn't a concerted effort to get the doors open, we were safe from any wandering zombies popping in on us that way...as long as nobody attracted their attention. I had to give him kudos for that.

"KL sent me back up. She told me to tell you to get going."

"Yeah, that sounds like her." I looked around us. The hallway was empty. "Is Jason where he's supposed to be?"

"He's watching Brandon, just like you told him to."

"And Carol Ann?"

"She's with Ann somewhere around here." She turned her head when someone hissed at her from below. The message was clear, they wanted her to hurry up. "I'm heading back down now. Don't worry. As soon as I see them coming my way, I'll unblock the door and let them in," she said. "Now shoo. You've got to watch them."

I ran back to the security room like my ass was lit on fire. It was time to ring the dinner bell and see how many zombies would show up for a free meal.

KL

Once we started down the stairs no one seemed interested in casual conversation, which was fine by me. My heart was pounding in true flight or fight mode and my hand itched for either an arrow or blade in it. I almost drew my sword but I wanted to keep my options open. I didn't want to be put in a situation where I'd have to drop the sword to nock an arrow. It was too narrow in the stairwell to do that, so I opted for the best compromise. One arrow tucked inside my fingers next to my bow and my sword arm still free to draw. That would have to do, that, and trusting my companions to work as a team.

Bobby had his war face on, which meant he was in battle mode. Eyes moving, watching everything and settling on nothing, his whole body as tense as a retriever on point. Actually, that wasn't quite right. It was more like a police dog waiting for the command to bite, and I hoped to God he was letting me pull his leash today.

Paul was sweating profusely and was starting to get a little funky, which meant the air around us was taking on a particularly pungent odor. The man needed to refresh his deodorant before he attracted insects, or something worse. Maybe funk was something that attracted zombies, a pheromone attractant that guaranteed you a date with the undead. I just wrinkled my nose at him and vowed to mouth breathe for as long as possible while we waited for Lauren to return.

Knowing Roxy, she would be up there chewing her nails and waiting until the last minute to leave, so I sent Lauren back up to check and tell her to get her ass in gear.

"Come on, Lauren. We need to get this show on the road." My whisper sounded loud in my own ears, but so did every foot shuffle and breath. I swore I could even hear the soft rasp of clothing rubbing against itself every time someone shifted position.

The stairwell was ugly, built out of utilitarian gray concrete blocks with concrete reinforced stairs that reminded me too much of a prison. The door was the same, its sheet metal exterior designed to keep fires from spreading and heavy duty enough to keep a small army at bay. It wasn't pretty like the areas meant for paying customers. Nice carpeting, fancy artwork, and water fountains were meant to entice and impress people that mattered, not the ones that had to work here.

Lauren popped her head over the railing and gave us a thumbs up before tapping down the stairs to join us. She had her ridiculously high heeled boots back on, newly relieved of zombie gunk thanks to a thorough washing in the breakroom sink.

"All set," she hissed, trying to stay quiet. The sibilant noise whispered up the stairwell and disappeared into the shadows above us.

I caught Bobby's eye then nodded towards the door. "Are we clear?"

There was a vertical window at head height that was too small to see much, unless you plastered your cheek against the reinforced glass. I let Bobby have the honors, then stood there hoping a zombie wouldn't try to kiss the glass on the other side and scare the crap out of everyone. He looked to the left and right, then stepped back. "I can't see a thing past the first open door, but we're clear up to there."

"Figures," I muttered.

"Okay guys. Remember, if you see any of them in the rooms, just try and shut the doors. No need to engage if we can trap them. All it will do is tire us out," I said, reminding them that this wasn't going to be the hard part of the game, this was just the warm up practice.

Paul and Bobby agreed.

"Ready?" I asked them.

"When you are," Paul said.

"Just get me to the escalator," Bobby said, pulling out his knife. His screwdriver was safely tucked away in his belt.

Lauren gave Paul one last hug, then pulled me in for a quick half-hug before I could protest. She grinned, and I shook my head at her. PDA was not my thing, and I was not a hugger in normal circumstances.

"Stay out of sight," I cautioned, then we were on our way.

Getting out the door went smoothly. The subtle snick of the door shutting behind us sounded like someone cocking a handgun. I glanced back to check on Lauren. Her face was visible through the glass. Pale with fear, she gave me one last wide eyed look before ducking away.

We headed for that first door and closed it without peeking inside. Bobby grabbed a chair and jammed it against the door, then Paul moved in with a length of blue cloth we had stripped from the curtains upstairs and threaded it through the door handles. A couple of quick twists and a tight square knot secured that room, and we were ready to move on.

There were only four rooms to secure, and we were starting to breathe a little easier after securing the first three without any altercations, then the fourth door decided to open all on its lonesome and we all froze mid-step.

Remember that old story about the tiger and the lady? Choose the right door and you find a beautiful woman behind it, choose the wrong one and a tiger jumps out to eat you? Well, our lady was a tiger, and none of us were sure what to do. She walked out of the room, a glorious cross-gender cosplay genius in leotards and a bright red cat head adorning her chest. An almost 6 foot tall neon orange tabby with wild hair and even wilder finger nails...and we stood there gaping at her until she turned and looked directly at us. I think until then we were all hoping she was still in the land of the living. Then she bared her teeth at us and the all too real feral cat hiss put that little idea to bed quicker than you could say "Oh, hell no."

She launched towards us and Bobby met her half way. At first I thought he had somehow ducked and shot past her, then she slowed down and fell to her knees. Paul jumped when her head bounced across his feet and kept going. He pulled his foot back as if he was going to kick the damn thing away, then stumbled back when tiger woman's teeth clacked shut and reopened so violently it sent one of her fake fangs shooting out of her mouth. "Shit!"

"Forget her," I growled. "Get the door before anything else comes out!"

Paul managed to get the door closed and tied down faster than a world class calf roper. He was still breathing hard when he came back to examine tiger woman. The jaw kept working furiously, the muscles bunching beneath rapidly paling skin as blood pooled beneath it. It sounded like she was chewing rocks, and I shuddered when I realized what I was hearing. With every bite, she—it was grinding her teeth hard enough to crack them.

"What the hell is that all about?"

"I don't know," I said, gingerly pushing the head away with the tip of my bow. "It's like a freaking snapping turtle." They would keep snapping long after you killed them. We would always bury the heads back when I was a kid, deep enough to keep the family dog from digging it up. If you didn't, you'd inevitably have to pull it off a lip or nose, and your pup would have to explain why he looked like a failed body modification experiment.

"Or a snake," Bobby added. He bent over the body and wiped his blade clean before joining us. He stared down at the head, then punted it down the hall before looking at me. "How long do you think it will do that?"

"I haven't got a clue, just try to keep your toes clear of it, that's for sure." I was impressed with Bobby even though it was freaking me out just a little. What was it about killing something that made him chatty? He had dispatched the furry formerly frozen without a single sound, and now he was standing here as calm as all get out and acting like we were hanging out at a bar and discussing sports...or the weather. The man was seriously messed up, but as long as he was being so handy with that knife I could forgive him that little eccentricity.

Sudden static from the speakers made me look up. I waved at the camera then grinned at my companions. "I think Roxy's trying to tell us to hurry up."

Despite the urge to move quickly, we slowly and carefully proceeded down the hall toward the escalator until we stood at the second floor landing. A quick peek over the railing showed us exactly what we were expecting to see—more than a few zombies wandering around aimlessly, and some doing unmentionable things I wish I could forget. Let's just say it would be a while before you'd hear me say I wanted a rare steak for dinner.

Once we left the relative safety of the hallway we'd be out in the open. The only cover we had was the railing, and we did our best to avoid attention. Bobby crawled the last few feet with his screwdriver between his teeth, pausing at the down escalator for a few long seconds before moving on to the up elevator. I felt Paul tense next to me and watched him grip his makeshift spear even tighter. The air around us seemed to gain a physical presence that made me all too keenly aware of the time as we waited for something to happen.

Very carefully, Bobby began to unscrew the plate in front of the escalator, stopping frequently to peek over the edge while the stairs continued their folding path before disappearing into a small opening at the top. The minutes ticked by so slowly I swore we were moving backward in time. Finally, he shifted to the side and popped the heavy metal plate out of its frame and slid it off onto the carpeting, leaving a gaping hole at the stop of the stairs that dropped off into a void. The sound of machinery click-clacking along was louder, but not so much that we thought the zombies would notice.

Bobby wiggled his way back to us and we were off. Just one more escalator to go and we could get back to safety, at least for a little while.

We repeated the same nerve wracking procedure on the second set of escalators, only this time it didn't seem to go so easy for Bobby. He was either getting tired, or someone had cross threaded a couple of the screws, because his face was getting red and he kept biting his lip to keep from cursing. You could feel the frustration coming off of him in waves, and that may be why he wasn't paying attention as well as he should have been.

All of a sudden Bobby rolled away from the metal plate and tried to stand up. He moved a hell of a lot faster than I thought anyone could, but he didn't even make it to his knees before it was all over.

Duly warned, I looked up just in time to see a zombie coming off the escalator after Bobby. He didn't grab the railing like a live person would have so he stumbled when he hit the top, but that wasn't what sent him sprawling.

"Damn, right in the eye," Paul whispered, sounding a little awestruck.

I just nocked another arrow and nodded towards Bobby. He was emitting a tightlipped high pitched noise that might have been a purposefully muffled scream, while his arms were busy trying to push the motionless zombie off his legs.

"Help him get that plate off before we get more visitors, won't you?" I could hear my voice through the blood rushing past my temples. I sounded so blasé, almost bored, and I felt my lips shape themselves into a pleasant smile. Why? Bobby had proven himself to be more human than I had given him credit for and the zombies had proven to be, well, standard in one respect...a brain shot stopped them cold in their tracks. It was good to know, and I filed that little tidbit of information away for future use.

Paul nodded and rushed to Bobby's aid. They managed to roll the now dead zombie onto the down escalator and I mourned the loss of one of my arrows as it thumped down the stairs with zero aplomb. The makeshift shaft had flown quite well, better than I had expected, and I couldn't have been more pleased. The sword was awesome and I wouldn't part from it easily, but I was glad I chose to keep the bow ready. It was my alter ego's choice of weapon, but I wasn't the Revenant Chaser, I was just KL. The bow was my weapon of choice and I had the trophies back home to prove it...plus one zombie.

That would be Rule Number 7: Know your weapons. When you are in the middle of a fight is not the time to learn.

Roxy

Sitting behind a computer desk and watching other people risk their lives is hard, sitting and watching someone you love do the same is even worse. My finger kept inching towards the loud speaker button, measuring the distance between the keyboard and the button like a chronic alcoholic trying to practice for the inevitable drunk test and hoping motor memory will be enough to get them through.

Why yes, officer, I can touch my nose with my finger, thank you very much. Do you want me to sing my ABC's, too?

The stray thought made me laugh, but the scenes playing out on the screens sobered me quickly. Badly pixilated and silently rolling in heavily washed out black and white, there was no early movie making campiness, no over the top close-ups of terrified women cowering beneath poorly made up movie monsters to offer comic relief. That stuff oozing out all over the carpeting wasn't chocolate syrup, and that wasn't a soccer ball they were kicking around. Those weapons were real and so were the zombies.

I have to say that having no sound actually made it worse. The soundtrack playing in my head was a veritable cornucopia of artistic license especially since I was forced to make it up as we went along. For the first time in my life, I was cursing the creative streak that let my imagination run so wild.

The half full bottle of whiskey we had taken from Jason sat just at the edge of my vision. A distracting bit of rich color in this shadowed booth of a room, it kept drawing my eye away from the task at hand.

"I hate whisky," I muttered, mentally giving Jason a free pass for breaking into the nasty stuff earlier. If it had been me sitting here all that time and watching the beginnings of the end of the world as we knew it, I might have been tempted to throw down a few shots myself.

My eyes burned from staring at the screens in front of me. I struggled against every blink. What I really needed was a cup of coffee, not because I was tired, but because I was too wired from the adrenaline overload. Caffeine seemed a better energy choice while I still had one. I had a feeling I was going to need those reserves of adrenaline before the day was through.

The air pressure changed behind me and I swung my head around just far enough to identify my visitor.

"Hey, how's it going?" Ann spoke in hushed tones, much like someone would do if they were talking during church services or at the theater.

"So far so good," I answered, my eyes plastered back on the screens like they should be. "Where's Carol Ann?"

It was her job to keep an eye on our strange little girl.

"She's playing with Brandon."

"What? How the hell is she playing with Brandon? He's tied up." I could hear her moving behind me. She stopped next to my chair and leaned against the desk to get a closer look at the screens.

"She doesn't seem to care. She's having quite the animated one sided conversation with him." She chuckled evilly. "He doesn't seem to be enjoying all the attention. She keeps whispering in his ear, then he starts to look like he's about to throw up. It's very amusing to watch him try to crawl across the room like an overgrown inchworm. I guess he doesn't care for kids very much?"

I shrugged. "I have no idea, maybe. But what about Jason? He's supposed to be watching him."

"He is, sort of. He's sitting at the desk playing solitaire on his phone," Ann admitted after a moment's hesitation. Was she worried about ratting him out? Jason had gone all tongue-tied on her when they met, but she hadn't seemed interested. Before I could decide whether I cared enough to find out if anything was brewing between them, all hell broke out in front of me.

"Shit!" I stood up so quickly the chair went flying out behind me, barely missing hitting Ann in the knee.

"What's going on?"

"That is the beginning of our exit strategy," I said. My eyes were glued to the action playing out on the screen in front of me. "I hope you can run in those shoes, because it's going to get mighty interesting in a few minutes."

Bobby and Paul got the last plate free and pushed it out of the way, then stumbled out of the camera's view a few steps in front of KL. She looked up at the camera and gave me a thumbs up and took off after them.

"Why did they do that? Take the escalator apart like that?" Ann asked, pointing at the spot where the heavy metal plates used to be.

The cameras were mounted high on the walls, giving me a bird's-eye view of the second floor landing as well as the first floor beneath it. Unless you were standing right at the edge of the access plate, you wouldn't even know it was missing. You also wouldn't notice that it wasn't just a free drop into nothingness down there. The metal stairs folded on themselves at the top, only to disappear into a mechanical monster that wasn't meant to be shared with anything else.

With deliberate slowness, the escalator marched not just up but around, a people moving conveyor belt armed with teeth and powerful gears that was just as hungry as the zombies trying to hitch a ride. With the smell of fresh blood drawing them in, a line of zombies bumbled their way up the moving stairs, much like the first one had before KL dispatched it with a well-placed arrow, only this time there was nothing solid at the top.

KL appeared on another camera, moving stealthily past the doors they had secured earlier.

"You might want to go find Carol Ann. They're almost to the stairwell." I turned to look at Ann. She hadn't even heard me. Even against the faint bluish gray glow of the screens you could tell her face had gone as white as a sheet. There was such a look of horror there. The kind that catches you, body and soul, and prevents you from looking away, even when you want to. I shook her arm and then resorted to pulling her away forcibly when she just stood there like a lump. "Blink, woman. I don't have time for hysterics."

A second before I resorted to slapping her she did blink, then she looked at me like I was the monster and started to shake. "Is that what you sent them out to do? I thought you were trying to disable the escalators to keep them from coming up here."

Her voice kept getting higher with each word, until it felt like my ears were going to bleed from the pitch. "Oh? How did you think we were going to disable a damn escalator? Turn it off? They obviously can still walk up stairs. We were actually counting on it."

"But, that...that's just inhumane," she cried, her gaze slipping back to the carnage on the screen before shuddering and clapping her hand over her mouth. "I think I'm going to be sick." The words were muffled, but the intent was clear from how hard she was trying to swallow.

"Don't you dare," I yelled. If she vomited, so would I. "First of all, they aren't human, so it can't be inhumane. Secondly, every one of those things that we dispatch is another one we don't have to wade through to get out of here. You don't have to like it, but that's the way it is."

"But..."

"No buts. We needed a diversion and that..." I pointed to the screen again, forcing her to look at what we had done to keep us all safe, then gave up being nice. I was pissed. She hadn't had to go out there and risk herself, and now she had the audacity to question our methods.

"That...they are our diversion. You need to stop worrying about them and start worrying about those of us who are still part of humanity and get your ass in gear. I need you to get the hell out of here, get Carol Ann in hand, and be ready to move when I say so, because otherwise you aren't going to get out of this place alive."

I turned my back on her and she fled from the room without another word. My job wasn't done yet.

I wasn't free to leave the security room, not until Bobby, Paul and KL were safely back in the stairwell.

"Well, Ann...you got one thing right. That certainly is a sickening sight," I muttered. Even for me, it was hard to stomach, and I'd seen some downright awful things in the past. Horrible things, wounds and injuries that should have killed a person but failed to do so. It was the sounds that they made while they begged for relief from the pain that had stayed with me the longest.

That was all in the past now, but the memories were still there. They protected me from the worst of the shock while I watched what looked like human beings disappearing into a gaping maw of live machinery only to be torn into bloody bits and pieces. The fact that they didn't scream, that they didn't seem to acknowledge any pain when limbs were torn from their bodies made it surreal to me. I could handle the carnage...as long as I didn't see terror and desperation in their eyes while it happened. Maybe that made me special, or perhaps it just made me a little more jaded than I cared to admit, but I was glad for the experience now.

Still, there was no reason for anyone else to have to watch. As soon as they were clear I turned off the offending monitor and headed out the door, eager to see my wife again. I knew she was safe, but I had to see her with my own two eyes before I could truly breathe a sigh of relief. I didn't know I was going to walk into another shit show, or that our brief respite was going to be whittled down to mere minutes.

As soon as I walked into the office, four pairs of eyes turned towards me and one pair turned away in guilt. KL's face was a thunderstorm waiting to happen.

"Where the fuck is Brandon?" she asked, her voice dark with promised violence. She took one step to the left, exposing an empty space where our errant team member had been deposited, and narrowed her eyes at Jason.

This wasn't the happy, triumphant reunion I was expecting.

"That's a very good question. Jason, would you care to answer that?"

KL

You could have heard a cricket fart.

Everyone stepped back, leaving a schoolyard fight tunnel between him, me and Roxy. Nervous glances were exchanged in the absolute silence following Roxy's question, leaving it up to me to find out what the hell happened.

"I will ask you one more time, Jason. Where the fuck is Brandon?" Roxy asked, her voice as cold as winter ice and just as sharp. He managed to look surprised, pale ginger eyebrows climbing almost to where his hairline ought to be if he didn't keep his head cleanly shaven, but I could tell he wasn't happy being called out. He drew himself up to his full height before answering, then managed to pitch his voice in such a condescending tone it made my hackles rise. I shook my head in disappointment at the obvious posturing. He should have known better.

"He had to take a piss so I let him loose," Jason said, looping his thumbs into his belt and rocking back on his heels. "He said he'd be right back."

"And you believed him?" I drawled, laying on the sarcasm thicker than peanut butter before glancing over at Bobby. He nodded and headed out the door without me having to say a single word.

"Why the hell didn't you go with him?" Roxy fired her question on the tail end of mine. Unlike me, she actually expected an answer.

"I wasn't going to take him to the bathroom," Jason grimaced. It was the same disgusted expression you would expect if you asked someone to do something gross, like jump in a cesspool.

"Holy shit. Are you afraid you might have had to see his wiener? I mean, come on. It's not like you would have had to shake it for him. I can't believe you. We were risking our lives down there so that we could all get out, hopefully in one piece, and you fucked up your only job." I was thoroughly disgusted with him at this point.

Bobby slipped back into the office and took his place again.

"Any luck?"

Bobby shook his head. "No. He's not in the bathroom that's for sure."

"Shit," Roxy muttered.

"I knew we couldn't trust him," I said, then pointed at Jason and sneered. "Your downfall was a penis. What would you do if a half-naked zombie came after you with its junk waving in the wind? Cover your eyes and run like a little girl just in case flaccid zombie dick might rub against you? Seriously, I really thought we had gotten past this homophobic shit. All you had to do was go with him and watch him pee."

"Shit, Jason, we did that every other day back in the Army. It's not that hard," Roxy muttered.

I smirked then, there was no way I could have managed to say that with a straight face.

Roxy turned her back on him, dismissing him as effectively as any dressing down. I was sort of surprised that she hadn't gone off on him, but there was obviously something else going on inside that head. A troubled glance around the room paused at Carol Ann, then continued to swing about until she stopped at me. Dead serious eyes caught mine, their normally bright cerulean hue now carried the subdued quality of storm darkened seas. "We need to go look at those cameras again."

That look and her statement sent alarms off in my head. My spine tingled and every nerve in my body woke up and stood at attention. The shit was about to hit the fan, and I had a feeling we were about to find out what it felt like to be the blades.

"You don't think we should search the floor first?" I asked. There was always hope he had just gone to ground and was hiding until we left.

"No. I have a feeling it's going to be a waste of time, time we don't have to waste," Roxy stated flatly, then walked past me and headed for the door.

For some reason Carol Ann came up and took my hand. When I looked down at her she smiled at me. "It's going to be okay, Revenant Chaser, uh...KL." She stumbled over the correction but then beamed up at me with such pride over remembering to use my real name I had to return that irresistible smile. I had no idea what that was about but I let her keep my hand as we all followed Roxy back to the booth.

She flipped the cameras back on and started scrolling through the screens. The escalators popped up, and I was distracted for a moment by the scene we had created. The camera angles and height didn't hide a thing. It was gross and disgusting and just as effective as we thought it was going to be as one by one, the formally frozen stumbled and fell into what I could only compare as a giant meat grinder. There was a rapidly growing dark stain oozing out along the first floor carpeting and the ones who weren't on their way up that little stairway to hell were falling to their knees at the edges of that shallow black lake.

I shuddered and turned away at the sight of several dozen zombies licking wet carpet, their faces smeared with the same dark shade of ooze. There was no way to pretend that dark stain was just water, not after seeing them rooting around in the pile of bodies like feral pigs who've turned on their pen mates. I nudged Bobby and nodded towards the cameras.

"If we manage to survive this with any amount of civilization left intact, the psychiatrists are going to have a field day," I whispered. "If there are any left."

He took a quick look then grinned at me. "Lines out the door and happy pills for everyone."

Gallows humor at its best, his response made me bite my lip before I succumbed to highly inappropriate laughter...the kind that makes you giggle when someone cracks their funny bone or falls over their own feet and everyone else looks at you like you're the biggest ass in the world.

"Shit, I knew it." Roxy stood up and tapped the offending screen. The door to the stairwell on the first floor was flung wide open.

"How did he get to the stairwell?" Paul asked.

"He must have been hiding, when we came back up, he snuck out behind us." Bobbie's explanation made the most sense.

"Hey, guys?" Ann broke in on our conversation. "Weren't you worried about Zombies climbing stairs before?"

"I guess so," I said, thinking about the escalator. They weren't exactly climbing the stairs there, all they had to do was step onto the first plate and they were on their way. "They're awkward, but..."

"Muscle memory. We spend most of our life on our feet...so they know how to walk without having to think about it," Lauren said. "Running or climbing is pretty much the same."

Four heads swung around to look at the screen again. A couple of the zombies had wandered into the stairwell and were starting to crawl up them after a few painful looking knee bangs against the first stair.

"What the hell did Brandon do? They shouldn't be interested in coming up here unless they heard or smelled something to draw them in," Lauren piped up.

"That doesn't matter now. We need to get that door secured before they find their way up here."

I had to agree with Roxy, but first I had to get the last word in just in case we weren't around later on to do it.

"Look what you did," I grabbed Jason by his shirt and pulled him closer to the screens. It didn't matter that he outweighed me by a good 100 pounds, I was pissed and he was too stunned to play the stubborn mule and pull back. I wanted to make sure he saw what he'd done...and what that meant to us all. "That was our way out."

I let him go and turned my back on him. I didn't want to hear any apologies or excuses. I was over him. Because of him Brandon had escaped and put the rest of us in danger. If we couldn't figure another way out of here, we were screwed.

Dealing with Brandon set my next rule, and it was one I wouldn't forget soon. It certainly wasn't one I would repeat.

Zombie Hunting Rule Number 8: Don't keep the coward alive out of some misplaced hope they'll turn around. They will just fuck you over the first chance they get.

That's exactly what Brandon had done. He didn't just leave. He left and didn't secure the bottom stairwell so now a bunch of zombies were blocking our planned escape route. That just brought douchebaggery to an entirely different level.

"Lauren, do you still have that block you used to secure the second floor door?" I asked. A plan was starting to form in my head, but for it to work, we couldn't have the second floor run over with zombies.

"Yeah. Why?"

"Just grab it and come with me. Paul, I need you to come with us. Jason and Bobby...I need you to find anything you can that's big and heavy and start stacking it in the hall."

"What do you want me to do?" Roxy asked, stepping in closer to me.

I lowered my voice, but not enough to prevent everyone from hearing me. "I need you to make sure they don't block the door before we get back." My paranoia was running in high gear and Roxy was the only one I could really trust. I handed her my bow and pulled off the arrow case. "There isn't enough room in the stairwell for this and you might need it. Just stay clear of the guys and let them do the grunt work. If anything other than us comes through the door, shoot it."

"You got it." Roxy hung the case across her back and nocked an arrow. She wasn't as good as I was with the bow, but this was close work and she routinely practiced with me. Giving her the bow evened the odds in her favor. That door would be unblocked and ready for us when we returned.

"Good. We'll be right back," I promised. The subtle hiss of steel being drawn made that promise sound more deadly, then we were back down the stairwell. The creepy crawly sensation of déjà vu hitched a ride on my back as we ran down the stairs. The metal and concrete vibrated beneath my boot heels, and I swear the damn zombies responded to it like a sonar ping. They looked up, saw us coming down to the second landing, and it was on. Like dangerous babies learning how to walk for the first time, they started up the stairs eagerly, lurching and falling as they went but becoming more proficient with every step.

"Hurry!" I hissed, holding the sword ready to swing at the first zombie to get in range. Lauren crouched down beneath us and jammed her makeshift block against the doorframe then stuffed a smaller block between the handle and the door so nothing could depress the lever. The uniquely sticky sound of duct tape followed. Smart woman.

"Done. Let's go!"

Lauren ran up the stairs and I had just turned to follow her when I heard Paul grunt. One of the zombies had made it up the stairs, mouth agape and broken teeth oozing blackish looking blood, his hands curled into claws that swiped out at Paul but missed. He didn't stay there for long. Paul grabbed the hand rails and swung out, hitting the zombie with both feet and kicking as hard as he could. The zombie, dressed in vibrant red, white and blue spandex, flew backward. It made airtime all the way down to the next landing, where it took out half a dozen other zombies.

If they had been real people, there would have been a few groans...the sound of air whooshing out of lungs like rookie wrestlers being tossed against the ropes in a free for all, but there was nothing. We heard the wet sound of bone under skin hitting something harder than it, the spray of blood splatting against concrete, and the whisper of cloth as they struggled to free themselves. That was the only sounds they made...that, and the sound of teeth gnashing and grinding against each other.

"Move, move, move!" Paul grabbed my shoulder and pushed me in front of him.

A few seconds later and we were back on the third floor. The metal door banged shut behind us and Bobby and Jason pushed us out of the way. We were all breathing hard and running on adrenaline so we let them take over. I found a wall and slid down to the floor, my sword on my lap and heart still pounding like a drum from the close call. Paul slid down next to me, breathing even harder. His nose whistled every time he exhaled, and I started to giggle.

"What's so funny?"

"I can hear you breathing, you sound like a whistle pop." That was where I was at. The sound of someone breathing meant the other person was still alive, which meant you could breathe easier.

"What's a whistle pop?" he asked.

I started laughing even harder. Paul looked at me like I had lost it...but I just waved him away. I had forgotten how young he was. I wasn't even sure they made whistle pops any more. "I'm okay. Really, I am. Just give me a minute."

"Not a problem."

He seemed perfectly happy sitting there for a few minutes. I reached over and patted his shoulder then leaned my head against the wall again. I wasn't ready to move just yet. "Thanks back there. You did well."

Jason and Bobby were stacking desks against the door frame. I'll admit it was a little overkill, but I wasn't going to put my ass on the line by assuming they couldn't do something...or remember how to do something. What was it Lauren had said earlier? Muscle memory. I wasn't going to bet any of our lives on the off chance one of those things wouldn't remember how to open a door and just walk on in.

Ann was off to the side with Carol Ann, keeping her close and out of the way.

"Did you see Brandon?"

"No," I said, not adding what I had seen of Brandon. The asshole hadn't been lying, he did need to take a piss. As much as I would have enjoyed learning the jerk was suffering from a bladder infection...the pinkish tinge of the small puddle I almost stepped in on the landing answered one question I had...his piss had attracted the zombies. I sent a fervent request out into the ether. If Mother Nature were kind to me she'd make sure it felt like he was pissing fire. Maybe she could add a really painful kidney stone just for fun.

"I don't understand why he would leave. We're safer as a group," Ann said.

"He doesn't care about the group. He only cares about himself." I was so over Brandon. I didn't care what he did or what happened to him at this point.

Jason and Bobby had finished blocking up the door just in time. The first zombie crashed into the door, then plastered itself against the glass window. Jason jumped back and almost fell over Bobby. Bloody spittle smeared across the glass, then a rhythmic tapping started. "Fuck, that's creepy. What's it doing?"

"I'm going to assume it's trying to eat through the door," I smirked, verses of Poe's *The Raven* running rampant inside my head. How damn appropriate was that?

"I'm really sorry," Jason muttered. He couldn't keep his eyes off of the door.

"I don't need a sorry, I need you not to fuck up when our asses are on the line." I wasn't going to let up on him now. This lesson was going to get beat into him while we were relatively safe so I didn't have to worry about him when it got ugly...and we were really close to approaching so much ugly it would make the worst slasher movie look like a ketchup spill.

"Remember tiny ears," Lauren spoke gently, reminding us that we had a child in our mist.

I looked over at Carol Ann. She didn't look traumatized by the zombies, let alone a little foul language. I just shrugged. "It's the fucking zombie apocalypse, Lauren. If she's sticking with us, I'm sure she's going to hear...and see a hell of a lot worse."

Then I stood up and dusted off my pant legs. It was time to prepare for a lot worse.

Roxy

Well, this was going to be a giant cluster fuck. After all the work KL, Bobby and Paul had done so we could go out the back easy-peesey, we were now left with no option but to go out the front.

My attitude was wavering somewhere between oh, shit and what the hell. I couldn't get that tiny little voice in my head to stop singing "You are so FUBAR'd" to the childish tune of Na-nah-na-nah-na-nah. That was how it felt. Things were definitely heading well past fucked-up-beyond-any-recognition, and every single person walking in front of me seemed, if not gleeful, at least resigned...to the fact that the reality train had departed without us despite the fact we had all paid for lifetime tickets.

"You know we're going to have to take the elevator now," I told KL, holding her back from the rest of the group. For my trouble all I got was a withering look and an over the top eye roll. Served me right, too, for pointing out something so painfully obvious.

"No shit."

"Okay, just checking." I left just enough doubt in my voice to let her know I was still worried. She just shook her head and gave me a lopsided grin that didn't match the solemnity in her voice.

"Right now I just want to get out of here alive. I will deal with how I feel about the box of death once I'm in the truck," she said, her lips twisting wryly before speaking too softly for the rest of the team to hear. "To be perfectly honest, I didn't think about that particular problem at the time. I just wanted to make sure we didn't end up overrun by zombies. This is really screwed up. We're basically treed up here. A juicy little raccoon family staring down at a pack of wild dogs. As much as I hate the idea of climbing inside that elevator again, I'm just glad we have the option."

"It's only for one floor," I reminded her.

"Ha! That's not what I'm worried about. It's not how far we have to go, it's how much empty space is beneath us that bothers me."

"You've watched too many horror flicks," I said, remembering too many late night movie's that involved just that sort of vertical bloodshed. Decapitations and fiery falls into midnight ink nothingness were just a few of the ways fictional characters have gotten the shaft to supply anxiety generating gore just for gore's sake. It's glorious onscreen when you know it's fake. Real life? Not so great.

KL crossed her arms and harrumphed at me. "Really? You do remember there's a shitload of zombies outside that door?"

"You've got a point," I admitted right before we stopped in front of the elevator. Our little band of misfits was standing ready, all decked out in whatever makeshift weapons they had managed to cull from the most boring aspects of corporate America.

"What the hell are those, Jason? We're not going after vampires." KL laughed at the big man standing behind Lauren and Carol Ann. Jason was something of a gym rat. His weapons seemed frail and pencil like in his hands, but they were sharp and he was strong...they would do the trick.

He held out what looked like a dowel, maybe 2 feet long, and spun it around in his hand before making a jabbing motion with it. "Believe it or not, this used to be a toilet plunger. Bobby found it in the bathroom and let me use his knife. I'm trying not to think about what kind of germs this thing has on it, but I'll gladly share them with one of those undead things out there."

"That's fine. Just remember to aim for the head, not the heart, if you want to stay alive," I reminded him, then turned back to KL. "Listen. I need to do something in the security room right quick, then we'll head out. Stay here and keep everyone sane until I get back, okay?"

"Do you need me?"

"Nope. Just forgot something I wanted to pick up. I'll be back before you know it."

Back in front of the TV monitors I couldn't resist pausing for a short minute and scanning every screen.

177

"Come on, you little rat-bastard, where are you?" I growled, then smacked the table hard enough to make my palm sting. My frustration had let me get distracted and I couldn't afford that. Pure dumb luck had provided us with a sneak peak of whatever we were walking into and it would be stupid not to take advantage of it. If we were going to step into hell, we would do it with as much intelligence as I could glean from these shaky images.

The first thing I noticed was that there were too many zombies stumbling around the base of the escalators, which was exactly what we had wanted maybe a half-hour ago. There was also a hazy quality to a couple of the screens that troubled me. My mind went back to Flambeau and his amazing blazing glory, just before we put his lights out for good—courtesy of a handy fire extinguisher. "One problem at a time, Roxy, one problem at a time."

There wasn't anything else to see, and only one more thing to do now...standing here was doing nothing but procrastinating. I spun around and almost took out Jason's bottle of whiskey. It fell and rolled across the table towards me, flashing bright accents of gold color that reminded me of something. "Hell, yeah."

I grinned and started pulling off the bug out bag, then started shuffling through the contents before tossing some of the sillier items out on the floor. Seriously, who thought you would need an emergency whistle or a comb? Shampoo?

"Jesus. Who packed this thing? Troop Beverly Hills?"

I kept digging until there was enough room for the bottle and a couple of other items I thought might come in handy and zipped the pouch shut, then checked my handiwork. It was nestled quite cozily in a cocoon of emergency dressings and bandages. All of that wouldn't keep it from breaking if I landed on it, but at least I wouldn't end up digging broken glass out of my ass for a week.

Two steps away from the door I had to mentally smack myself on the forehead for almost forgetting the one thing I promised to do before we headed out. The CD case was right there next to the stereo, all ready and waiting for me. A row of on/off switches were conveniently labeled and I went through them carefully...the ones I had switched to on when we were working on Plan A were now safely switched off. My finger paused over the power button, then I closed my eyes and smiled before hitting the button. "This is for you sweetheart. I promised you a soundtrack to fight zombies by, I hope you like my choice."

I couldn't hear the music playing, but the security screens told me everything I needed to know. "Dance, motherfuckers...dance until you can't dance anymore. Just dance away from me and mine."

Just for fun, I turned the volume dial as far as it would go, then slipped out the door. It was time to get the hell out of here.

KL

Roxy strolled back to the elevator with a pleased grin on her face. I was instantly suspicious but my curiosity had to wait.

"All ready?" she asked almost too cheerfully, then hit the button when we all nodded. No one spoke, it didn't seem to be the time for idle chatter. Nervous fingers checked their weapons, then moved to faces that suddenly itched from sweat pouring out of them. It was all nerves. The A/C was still working, but the air inside the box of death promised to heat up quickly from all the live bodies crammed into the small space.

Roxy was the first one in and I was the last. She held the door open for me and waited. She blocked the door when it tried to close and I could hear it fighting against her, the metal sheathing vibrating with the effort. I would have liked to have said that the mind was willing but the body was fighting back, but it would have been a lie. Body and mind were in perfect harmony with each other. They were stubbornly refusing to move forward until Carol Ann squirmed out from under Ann's arm and ran to me.

"Come on, KL. We're all waiting on you," she said, taking my hand. She said it like I was

181

important, not like I was afraid, and that made me feel better. I looked down at her and she beamed up at me. Her small, round face looked so normal...so much like many of my friends' kids at her age, that I almost forgot about the video. I wasn't sure if knowing that she wasn't normal should make me feel better or worse that she showed so much trust in me.

"Carol Ann?" I crouched down so we were face to face. "What do you want from me?"

"Silly," Carol Ann giggled, covering her nose and mouth to hide her small, straight teeth before leaning closer to me. She slid her eyes to the side, all sly like, and giggled again. She tried to whisper but it was the childish sort of whisper that told you their voices hadn't learned enough control to hide what they were thinking. "To save all of us, just like you're supposed to do."

She must still have me confused with The Revenant Chaser.

She giggled again, then threw her arms around me and hugged me tightly. "Give me a ride?"

I couldn't refuse. We walked into the elevator and I tried to ignore my heart jumping into my throat when the doors closed and the box bounced beneath us before heading south. It was a smooth enough ride after that, lasting only a few moments...but the damn thing moaned like an unpaid whore the whole way down. It wasn't happy and neither was I.

To top it all off, Roxy kept humming something that sounded so damn familiar I could feel the name of it right on the tip of my tongue but I just couldn't quite catch it. The box of death stopped and bounced a little, then dinged merrily to announce our arrival. I rolled forward onto the balls of my feet. Just like a prize fighter responding to the referee's bell, I was eager to leave my corner and meet my opponent.

As soon as the door whooshed open I felt like I could breathe again. "Here, Ann, take her for me will you?"

I handed Carol Ann off, reluctantly drew my sword and headed out the door. There was only so many arrows in my quiver. The blade would have to do unless absolutely necessary, which sucked because it was a damned messy way to deal with things. An arrow was neat and tidy, and had the added benefit of keeping 20 feet or so between me and my target. Get ahold of my real arrows and that 20 feet went out to 30 or more. Get home and to one of my compound bows and I'd never have to get close enough to smell 'em, and that suited me just fine.

"What is that?" Ann asked, lifting her nose and sniffing.

"Smells like bar-b-que." Jason grinned and smacked his lips.

183

Jason was a Carolina boy, born and bred. He could smell a pig picking from a mile away. Hell, he probably kept a bottle of hot sauce in his glove box.

"That's just nasty, Jason." Roxy stuck her tongue out and made a fake retching noise. If she was really going to vomit, it sounded more like a cat hacking up a hairball, so I didn't bother moving aside.

"Why? Smells better than the cold pizza and stale PB&J's we had to eat earlier."

I ignored the not so subtle jab at the rules we had laid out upstairs, but Roxy didn't. "Uh, yeah. Except remember our flaming zombie? There might be a smattering of chicken tenders in the mix, but that smell you're drooling over? That's people."

Jason turned a lovely shade of green and swayed in his size 14 combat boots. At a good foot taller than most of the girls, he wasn't going to find much support if he decided to pass out. I had a feeling he was going to find out what it felt like when Jack cut down the beanstalk. Even with the carpeting that was going to hurt like hell.

"Dude, suck it up," I snarled, hoping to get a reaction from him. "You faint on us, I'm gonna leave your ass here."

Jason's Adam's apple bobbed furiously until he could swallow his nausea. "I wasn't going to faint."

"Of course you weren't," Bobby piped up, slapping Jason on the back and heading out. "Let's get the hell out of here."

We retraced our path from earlier. Lauren sidestepped around the headless pussy cat while Ann tried to position her body between the carnage and her small charge. Carol Ann seemed content to hold her hand and go wherever we were going, even if she did seem to insist on skipping the entire way.

"What the hell is she singing?" Paul weaved in closer to me to ask quietly.

I hadn't even noticed she was singing, but now that someone had pointed it out it was pretty obvious. I cocked my head and listened, then tripped over my own feet when I caught a couple of the lyrics.

Ring around the rosie, pockets full of posies...ashes, ashes, we all fall down.

"Do they still teach little kids that old ditty?" I asked, feeling death walk down my spine. I've always hated that nursery rhyme, with its connection to the dark ages and the plague. The Black Death had killed millions. Bodies had piled up so high they were forced to burn them before disease spread from their rotten corpses. Considering how fast bodies were piling up, the song had a sort of sick logic to it that was all the more disturbing coming from Carol Ann.

With temperatures in the high 90's during the day, any zombie sitting out in the sun was going to become a bloater, then a popper, terms we had affectionately come up with to describe those poor critters left on the side of the road after getting hit by a car. Usually raccoons or possums, they would slowly bake in the heat until they looked like Macy's Day Parade balloons. Then they would pop and it was Aliens all over again.

My feet started to move a little faster. I so did not want to be anywhere inside of a city in a couple of days.

"So far, so good." We hadn't had one single zombie greet us in the hallway. Rather than make me feel happy, it just made me twitchy. There was no way this was going to happen easy, that was just too much luck for one person.

"Hush, don't jinx us." Lauren narrowed her eyes at me and shook her head. She was a firm believer in full moon madness and always kept a four leaf clover in her wallet.

"I think it's too late for that," I smirked. She took a swipe at me but I was too fast and all she took out was empty air.

It felt good to joke around, but the mood didn't last long. The feeling of something bad happening got worse the closer we came to the escalator. I sheathed my sword and pulled off my bow. It just made me feel better having the more familiar weapon in hand. With nothing but the handrail to hide behind now, we were forced to crouch down. I could feel the escalator motor chugging away beneath my feet.

"Wait. Something doesn't feel right." I kneeled down and placed my hand down on the carpeting. The floor vibrated beneath my palm, but there was something else. A steady thumping bumped against my knee and fingertips. "Feel that? The escalator didn't sound like that before."

I looked back at Roxy and caught her smiling at me. She had that Cheshire cat, full teeth grin going on that always gave her away when she'd done something sneaky.

"What did you do?"

"I turned up the bass."

"Is this what you were humming earlier?" I asked, relieved as hell that the escalator wasn't suffering some sort of catastrophic failure.

"Highway to Hell," Roxy replied. "It was the best I could do."

"Seems appropriate." I had to smile at her choice. At least she hadn't lost her sense of humor.

That brings me to Rule Number 9: Even in the middle of a zombie apocalypse, humor is everything. No one wants to hang out with a Debbie Downer.

"I did promise you music to slay by." Roxy winked at me then turned to pop a glance over the railing. "Wonderful. I've got the music pumping in the main hall and AC/DC is working as a great pied piper. We've lost at least half of the zombies down there. Ann? You and Carol Ann stay in the center.

Everyone else spread out but stay close. Leave swinging distance."

Roxy moved up by my side and Paul took the other with Lauren behind him. Bobby and Jason took the rear position.

We tried to move quickly but quietly toward the meat grinder...um, escalator. I didn't look, mostly because I knew where not to look, and partly because I knew what I would see if I did. A couple of the others weren't so lucky.

Someone whimpered behind me. It was Ann, someone I had considered one of the weaker links this morning, but who had managed to impress me more and more as the day progressed. You could tell she was terrified but was putting on a brave face in front of Carol Ann. Personally, I wasn't sure that Carol Ann was the one who needed the protection, which was a shame, because it was obvious that Ann would sacrifice herself to save that little girl. A saving she probably didn't need. In a world full of uncertainty there was one thing I was completely certain of...if only one of us made it out of here alive, it was going to be Carol Ann.

Someone started retching behind us, they had my full sympathy but not my attention. I didn't dare look behind me to find out who it was. It was one thing to view the carnage on a small black and white screen and another to experience it in all its 3D Technicolor goriness.

"Holy shit," Lauren whispered.

I was tempted to remind her of little ears but now didn't seem like the time.

"Holy shit is right."

Roxy

"Woohoo! Background music." KL pumped her arms in the air. She was way too excited about having a soundtrack, but I got it. More accurately, I got her and her need for music. It gave her that motivational kick that spilled out into the rest of the team. I saw backbones straighten and a renewed confidence chase away the fear in their eyes.

We had almost made it down the escalators before the shit hit the fan again. It was surreal. As we went down, the hungry faces of the formerly frozen followed us on their way up. A few tried to turn around on the moving stairs, bumping into the ones crammed in behind them. Suddenly one of them got smart. Instead of following behind, lemming like, it turned and lurched up the down escalator, then promptly face planted when the stairs didn't cooperate. The thumpa-thumpa noise it made each time its chin hit a stair competed with the bass throbbing through the Convention Center Walls. It was absolutely hilarious. So was its attempt to crawl back up towards us. It was basically going nowhere—the escalator had become a zombie treadmill. Unfortunately, it was blocking our way out and we were rapidly approaching a foot to head meeting.

191

A squealing noise on the left distracted me. One of the up escalator zombies had managed to climb over the rubber railing and onto the shiny reflective metal surface separating us from them and was sliding down the damn thing towards us. Now we were caught between one zombie above us and one below, on a down escalator that wouldn't stop moving.

"Get it, get it, get it!" Jason yelled, lunging for the thing's feet while Ann hugged the opposite side of the stairs, keeping Carol Ann as far away from the belly surfing zombie's hands as possible. He managed to catch a leg and pull back, but not before it slid far enough down to catch KL by the sleeve.

"Oh Hell, No." My heart leapt into my throat and I started running back up the steps. I needed to get close enough to help.

Before I could push past Lauren, KL swung her sword, bringing it straight down on its head. The blade rang out, and for a second I was worried the tip was going to snap off. The damn thing was stuck between its eyes like one of those rubber Halloween gag knives and KL couldn't get it free.

"Shit, that doesn't happen in the movies," she growled, tugging as hard as she could.

"Back up!" I yelled, quickly running out of steps to run up.

"I can't. It's stuck!" The blade bent even farther as the zombie corpse kept slipping down the impromptu slide.

"Ah, fuck it," I muttered. KL was in no danger from the up escalator zombie, but she needed time to get that blade free. Taking a move from Paul's playbook, I ran back down the stairs and with a hand on either rail, I kicked out and up with as much power as I could muster, managing a 10 point landing on top of the bottom floor zombie. I was now straddling the zombie, but facing the wrong way. What happened next was a glorious example of grace and ability that could only occur in a severely fear induced state and never on purpose.

If I had a rope, the zombie I was sitting on would have been hogtied and left to wither and die on its own...but all I had was the 180 pounds I was pushing and my ass to keep the damn thing face down on the floor.

"I got it, Roxy." Lauren ran up to me with the one and only weapon she had found up on the third floor. Her eyes met mine and I nodded, then grabbed a handful of greasy hair and yanked back hard enough to make my zombie assume a yoga pose I could have never mastered. His back arched underneath me, but before he could react, Lauren jabbed a ridiculously dangerous looking knitting needle right up its nose and wiggled it around in a tight circle. The zombie went limp. Lauren propped her foot against his shoulder, those long ass heels digging into the unfeeling flesh and yanked. The needle popped back out with a wet sucking sound suddenly enough that she stumbled into Paul.

"Thanks," I said, grateful to let go of the head and watch the now still body fall to the ground. Instead of a plain dull thunk, it landed with a heavy splash. It was only then that I noticed my pant legs were soaked at the knees and realized why they felt so sticky. My brain didn't want to process the reality of kneeling in a bloody carpet lined lake of zombie squish. My breathing sped up, but it was hard to hyperventilate when you were trying to breathe shallowly through your mouth.

"Gross," I muttered, more than happy to take Lauren's offered hand to stand up. It was either that, or push off the floor with my hands.

"A bit." Lauren cocked her head at me, grinning at me expectantly. "What? No pithy comment for me here?"

"Huh?" I had to admit I was lost there for a minute, then I looked down at our scrambled eggs for brains zombie and chuckled.

"A pithy comment for a not quite textbook pithing, eh?" I asked, raising an eyebrow. Leave it to Lauren to dig out an old Biology 101 joke after taking out a freaking zombie.

Lauren had just enough time to shrug, then her eyes flashed from humorous to serious in a quick second and we were too busy to joke around anymore.

"We've got to go, people." I heard Bobby's voice but didn't see him, then the familiar sound of an arrow being released buzzed above my head and a particularly nasty looking zombie arched backwards and lost its footing on the wet carpeting.

"I knew I should have snuck a machete or something in...but noooo, you wanted me to follow the rules."

"Okay, okay. I heard you the first time," I grunted, taking a swing at the nearest zombie's temple with my nightstick. The loud crack that followed was hollow, like tapping a really, really hard watermelon, but it did the trick and was oh, so satisfying. Sarcasm wasn't just a tool in KL's arsenal, it was a weapon, and she was being just as free with that sharp tongue of hers as she was with her blade. She bitched, I swung, and zombies fell. It worked.

"We'll be fine, you said. It's just a bunch of happy, nerdy people having a good time, you said." The litany of complaints continued. Timed to perfection with every swing, they turned the skirmish into performance art.

"Let's just get out of this building and you can tell me all the way home how wrong I was." I bashed another one of them in the head. This time it kept coming.

"Fuck!" The bastard grabbed my arm and yanked. I yanked back, then swung around and brought the nightstick down across its forearm. The

195

forearm snapped like a wishbone, bending at an unnatural angle that made me cringe, but didn't stop me from following up with a backhanded strike across the jaw. Teeth flew everywhere, then suddenly there was no zombie, and a poorly constructed jack-o'-lantern head tumbled away from us.

"Thanks babe." KL had just lopped its head off for me.

"Hit harder," she yelled. I don't know why she bothered yelling, she was standing right next to me.

"Easy for you to say, you've got the sharp pointy!" I wheezed, then coughed hard enough to make my lungs scream. It was starting to hurt to breathe, let alone yell. The smoky haze I had noticed on the security screens was thicker here and had a nasty chemical smell to it. I coughed again, my eyes starting to burn and tear up from the crap in the air. "We've got to get out of here, it's impossible to breathe in this shit!"

Everyone was doing what they could to fend off the zombies. Lauren was swinging the bugout bag around in a wild circle and taking out anything that Paul managed to knock down with that makeshift battle hammer he had duct-taped together. After my little demonstration she had found her inner warrior woman and was gleefully landing on the backs of anything that moved and slipping those metal needles inside one skull after the other...all 88 pounds of her. She looked like a child trying to ride a Clydesdale.

Who the hell knits with those things? Not only were they solid metal and at least a foot in length, they were connected by a thin cable about 40 inches long that made me think of garrote wire.

Bobby was just stabbing away with his big ass knife and Jason was doing his best to keep Ann safe. With the kid in her arms she couldn't defend herself and I was glad he had stepped up and taken charge of that situation.

"There's too many of them," Paul gasped.

"If you've got another plan, spit it out," I barked back, barely avoiding getting bowled over by a very large man in a full body Spiderman suit. At 400 plus pounds he looked more like Spidey and the Michelin Man's love child and there was no way I'd survive that tire rotation.

"Oh, that's just not right," Paul said. I had to agree.

It was all a slippery blur after that. KL yelled something, her voice harsh and demanding. I had to hold my breath to hear what she was saying, I had an ocean of blood whooshing past my temples and my lungs burned with a new kind of pain as they fought to keep up with my body's demands. "What?" I yelled, managing to sound more peevish than terrified.

"Ignore the one's in costumes! Just keep 'em off of you but don't waste your energy trying to kill them. They can't bite you through their masks."

"Well, fuck, why didn't I think of that?" I asked, fighting the urge to scream "Eat lycra, motherfuckers" and laughing maniacally.

After that bit of advice we were able to get some forward momentum going. We weaved, we danced, we did everything but double dribble our way through a path of slow zombies and before we knew it we were past the food court and headed for the glass doors that led outside and, we hoped, to freedom.

I doubled up my speed and ran straight for the door as fast as I could and I still managed to take up the rear. Sometimes being short sucked, like now. Other times it was awesome, like never needing to duck under trees and stuff like taller folks and always having room in the bed to stretch out. Hell, in a pinch a loveseat made a great bed, you didn't need a full size couch, but now? It just made me slower than everybody else.

Then KL was back beside me and everything was okay in the world again.

"You didn't think I'd leave you behind, did you? I'll always have your back, babe." KL's promise was delivered with that particularly rakish grin she could pull off like no other and which I loved to sketch.

KL was in full Revenant Chaser mode. Black
hat low on her forehead and blade swinging like
there was no tomorrow. She mowed through the
undead as efficiently as her alter ego dispatched
revenants in our comic books. Her quiver was empty
and I would bet my life that every one of those
arrows had hit their mark. Somewhere behind us
was a little forest of green fletched dowels standing
in testimony to her marksmanship skills.
Unfortunately, we had another forest to deal with
and it was ugly.

Twisted and burnt, they advanced on us from
the direction of the food court. Covered in blackened
skin and oozing wounds, they looked more like the
charred remains of trees than what they used to
be...living, breathing human beings. These were the
first zombies that actually looked like zombies,
sightless eyes shining milky white against
overcooked flesh that wept and crackled with every
step like an open bag of potato chips.

Head up, blindly sniffing the air like a dog, the
closest one suddenly went on point and bared its
teeth in our direction. Its lips cracked open and
started to bleed, streaming a bright red against
unnaturally white teeth that were too evenly spaced
to be real.

"Ugh, no amount of Chapstick is gonna fix
that," I muttered, stepping back into a defensive
posture and raising my baton in front of me. "What

do you think happens if a zombie bites you with its dentures in?"

"Let's try to not to find out." KL shook her head at me and gave me the look. The one that silently asked if you'd finally lost it, while simultaneously wondering how you managed to escape the funny farm in the first place.

Her obvious disdain at my curiosity left my next question stuck to the underside of my tongue where it would stay safely tucked away. Hey, I was a writer...it's not like I could control the questions that popped into my mind at odd times. But really, no one's ever asked...can you get zombified by getting gummed by a toothless zombie?

Inquiring minds want to know.

KL

So close.

Jason shook the exit doors so hard we could hear the chain wrapped around the handles rattle. He grunted from the effort, his face contorting into a ruddy mask of barely contained rage that I was too tired to feel.

Now I knew how those animals at the zoo felt, spending their days watching perfectly tasty humans being marched past the glass enclosures and knowing from experience that they couldn't reach them. So they paced, and watched, and dreamed of running, but never did because they never knew when nothingness would become somethingness that hurt like hell when you ran into it. Wild critters must really be confused as fuck about glass, and now it was our turn to beat against that invisible barrier. One quarter inch of solid nothingness stood between us and escaping.

"God dammit!" Roxy growled, taking a swipe at the glass door with her nightstick. The heavy steel tubing didn't even chip it. "I refuse to get this far just to die plastered against the edge of a giant fishbowl."

Leave it to humans to figure out a way to see nature but not have to deal with all the yucky parts of it, you know, like heat, cold, fresh air, mosquitos, etcetera, etcetera, then go even farther with the concept. Simply turning sand into an invisible shield wasn't sufficient. Glass was brittle, it shattered and broke into a million shards of uselessness until we figured out how to make it harder, stronger, and basically impossible to break.

"Paul?" Roxy waved him forward

"Sorry, I've got nothing." Paul held up his makeshift spear slash battle hammer and shook his head. The duct tape had held up admirably until the last wave hit us, now it was soaked in blood and shredded beyond repair. The Lucite trophy he had lashed to the end now hung loosely in its bindings, the impromptu weapons version of limp dick syndrome. Basically, it was now useless.

"What do we do now?" I asked, keeping an eye out for any more zombies. Several folding tables had been knocked on their sides and made a pretty good hiding place but I didn't expect them to protect us from a full on rush. "We're all wiped out. I'm out of arrows, and the only other way out I can think of is the delivery bay doors in the back."

My sword arm felt like Jell-O and the lightweight sword-cane was starting to feel like a full length double handed broadsword, intended for someone with Conan the Barbarian's muscles, not me. I wasn't sure how much longer I could lift it, let alone swing it effectively. Everyone else carried the same expression on their face that I was feeling all the way down to my bones. Exhaustion bordering on a total loss of hope.

"Yeah, well, thanks to Brandon that's not a viable option either," Roxy said.

"What about the other side? This place has two entrances, one on either side," Bobby asked, pointing back the way we had come with his long knife.

That involved backtracking past both sets of escalators. I thought about it, then discarded that idea. "If they locked these doors, I'm pretty sure they did the same there too."

"I don't get it though. Why are the doors chained shut? And who did it?" Ann asked.

"I don't know." I tapped the glass, just above the thick chains. There was a poster size notice stuck to the outside of the glass. "I don't recognize these symbols, but I'm pretty sure this place has been secured by someone we really don't want to meet. Homeland security, possibly. Maybe the CDC...but if they didn't even bother to check for people, they're more than likely the shoot first-ask questions later sort of people."

"But how did they know? The Con hadn't been open but maybe an hour or so when everything went weird. That's awful quick for the government to move in," Ann asked the group in general.

Good question, but I wasn't sure how important having the answer was at that moment. Continuing to breathe was.

"Hell, how do we know we're the first ones? This shit could have been happening for a while. Maybe in other places. Maybe they knew beforehand and were just waiting for orders to move out. I don't fucking know," Roxy said. Her face hardened and she looked about ready to eat through the glass in order to get out. "All I know is if we get the hell out of here and find Brandon, I'm going to kick his ass until he begs to be fed to the zombies, one damn limb at a time."

The fact that she used if instead of when set my teeth on edge. The rest of the crew sensed it too and they shuffled their feet, uncomfortably passing nervous glances between them. Bobby looked especially guilty.

"It's not just Brandon's fault. If we hadn't stuck around to look for Tommy, we might have gotten out," Bobby muttered.

"We don't know that. Hell, we could have walked into the middle of an entirely different sort of shit storm if we had left right away. I don't see anybody out there, do you?" I asked. The walkway was suspiciously clear of anything alive or moving and what I could see of the parking lot, it was still pretty full of cars—empty cars. "I find that kind of odd."

"Too many unanswered questions, and not a single answer for the one we really need. How are we going to get out of here?" Lauren stepped into the conversation.

Roxy shrugged. "There's always the food court. Most of the zombies there became crispy-critters when Flambeau set the place on fire. Maybe the smell will mask us and let us sneak into the main hall. We could still try to make it to the back loading dock."

I rolled my neck until it popped, trying to relieve some of the tension in my shoulders, and then looked to Roxy before nodding. "Agreed."

Damn, I was so not happy about this decision. Ann had slid to the floor and was trying to entertain Carol Ann by playing some sort of hand clapping game. Now she needed back up and I let Jason and Bobby handle it.

She moved with the dead tired shuffle of the homeless that littered the sidewalks of every major city in the United States. There was more to that shuffle than mere fatigue, it had to do with hopelessness and a rapidly narrowing reality that smacked you in the face with its stark lack of a safety net. Fall now, and you hit the ground beneath you hard.

"Ann?" Roxy asked gently. She had noticed it, too. "Can you keep going?"

Ann looked down at Carol Ann, then took a deep breath and nodded her head emphatically. "Yeah, I'll keep up."

"Just take care of Carol Ann. We'll handle the rest. Run if you have to run, okay?" I advised, knowing this was what she would do if it all went to hell and people starting dying, but at least this way she wouldn't have to feel guilty about leaving us. She didn't answer right away, just sniffled and wiped her eyes.

"Got it?" I asked again, this time reaching out and squeezing her shoulder. She looked up at me and nodded again. This time I could tell by the look in her eyes that she understood me completely. "Good. Now let's get the hell out of here."

Tears fell, but I pretended not to notice that she was silently crying. I didn't blame her. The definition of living had just changed remarkably. Just surviving didn't mean having enough money to make it through the month with all your bills paid, something that was a cause of celebration for too many people in our great nation. It now meant living long enough to make it to your next meal, then hoping it wouldn't be your last. If what was going on here was happening everywhere around the globe, humans had just defaulted on their longstanding claim that they were the top of the food chain. We were a paltry seven—eight if you included Carol Ann, and there were hundreds of zombies. Terrible odds that only served to illustrate the obvious. We were no longer the hunters, we were the hunted and not everyone would be able to handle that. You would be foolish to believe otherwise. Ann was too soft for this, but she had done what Brandon couldn't. She found a way to be brave, not just for herself, but for a total stranger. She was a good reminder of what humanity was all about...and for that...I would do what I could to keep her alive and well.

We made it pretty far. The entrance to the food court smelled like burnt rubber and other stuff better left unmentioned. We found a few zombies that weren't in any shape to attack anybody, melted together in a messy puddle on the floor in front of the sneeze shield. It was pretty gruesome. I didn't even want to know how hot it had gotten in here before the fire suppression system kicked in, but what was left was a pretty good approximation of what hell on earth would look like.

"Don't trust anything to be down for good in here," I cautioned, right after something I thought was too roasted to be able to move suddenly slid across the floor towards me and latched onto my ankle. A well-placed boot heel ended that one quickly, its skull crunching wetly onto the linoleum floor. "Don't get too close to them."

I guess that would be Zombie Hunting Rule Number 10: Never assume a zombie is dead meat unless you're the one that took it out.

Sweat startled to trickle down my back, adding to the itching sensation between my shoulders. Something was about to go bad, really bad. I could feel it.

Something loud banged in the kitchen, followed by the sound of cans falling. I swear I heard the walls creak, and the sensation of the building

207

taking in a deep breath and holding it made it feel like there wasn't enough oxygen in the room.

"Help!" Ann yelled, falling back on her heels and trying to scuttle away with Carol Ann in her arms. A half-dozen crispy critters had come from nowhere, splitting our group in half and leaving the least armed of us in the worst danger.

"Carol Ann, no!" Ann threw out her hand, but missed the little girl.

The little girl wiggled out of Ann's arms and stood in front of her, defiantly crossing her arms at the approaching zombies, using her small body as a shield. Her bottom lip pouted and she waggled one chubby finger at them and yelled. "NO! You will not hurt my friends!"

I started towards them, intent on taking out as many of the zombies as I could before they got to her, but I never got a chance.

Her eyes screwed shut and she yelled even louder. "Go away!"

I swear the zombies flinched, then I wasn't too sure. That subtle creak I was catching just at the edge of my hearing turned into a growl, then a deep rumble that shook the floor beneath us. Roxy stumbled and almost fell, then made it to me. Her grip tightened and I felt a tug at my sleeve.

"Move!" she yelled, "Run, now! Get back to the tables and take cover before it's too late!"

I didn't need to be told twice. Everyone hauled ass back the way we came, jumping wildly over zombies and other detritus littering the floor. Ann was managing to keep up with us, but only because Jason signaled her to pass Carol Ann. Ann passed her like a football and doubled down on her running, reaching the tables just in time for Paul to reach out and pull her down to the ground. Jason slid into a really small space for such a big man and curled up in a ball with Carol Ann tucked in the middle.

I got an image of zombies coming up right behind us, then suddenly they were airborne and so were we. It felt like a Mack truck hitting me across my shoulder blades and then we were skidding across carpeting that felt more like rough grit sandpaper working hard to scrape off the first layer of my skin before we stopped just shy of the outside wall.

"Ouch. What the hell?" I groaned, rolling over and reaching for my blade on my hands and knees. My ears were ringing and I felt nauseated, but I somehow managed to stand up and look around. There was smoke everywhere, and flames were licking at the entranceway to the food court.

Roxy coughed then turned and spit before checking herself. "Yuck, is everyone else intact?"

"It looks like it, thanks to you," Lauren said, smiling past a mask of sweat and black smoke lines streaked across her face. "What happened?"

"Structural damage. The fire must have damaged some of the beams above the food court and they finally gave way." I coughed. The smoke was getting worse and the fire was getting hot enough to feel from here. "A pipe or propane tank or something must have been hit and it exploded. We were damn lucky to have gotten out of there alive."

"Sheee-it," Jason drawled. He was equally covered in smoke, dust and bits of crispy critter that floated about on the hot air currents around us. "We're still in the same boat we were in earlier. We still can't get out."

"Actually, we do have a way out," Bobby piped up. We all turned to see him grin at us, then point straight up in a decidedly godly, churchy sort of way. I truly thought he had lost it until I rolled my eyes up to see what he was talking about. Some of the cables holding one of those beautiful life size statues of dolphins suspended above us had snapped. Flipper was no longer serenely swimming along the air currents high above our heads, it had taken a nosedive straight for the glass wall behind us and escaped the fishbowl. The glass was riddled with cracks all the way down to the base.

Roxy handed Jason her baton and gave him a tired salute. "You get the honors. Get us out of here and I'll get us home."

Roxy

We were finally out of the building but we weren't out of danger. Once we hit the parking lot we had to abandon the concrete walkway for the blacktop. It gave us more room and left more space between us and the cars. Besides, the sidewalk wasn't as empty as it had seemed from the entranceway. Bodies littered the otherwise pale concrete, each one marked by a rapidly drying blood stain circling their head like some perverted version of a halo.

"What the hell happened out here?" KL asked, turning around in a circle to take in all the carnage.

"Bullet hole," Bobby stated. "Just one, and a clean head shot at that." He kneeled by one of the bodies and used his knife to turn its head. Blank eyes stared up at the sky beneath greasy hair.

It was a scrawny looking kid with coke bottle glasses and a "this is my superhero costume" t-shirt. He couldn't have been more than 15 or 16. A few feet away a small group of teenage girls lay on the grass in a tight huddle, every single one of them clutching their phones in perfectly manicured hands. Even in death, not a single one of them was looking towards the little geeky dude.

Ann swallowed and turned away. She paled and looked like she might get sick. "Were they even zombies?"

"That's the thing, isn't it? We can't tell. If it was the fucking movies, they'd gray up and look dead...but real life doesn't do a magic makeup trick on the undead so you know who to spike," I said. "These folks could have been running towards a meal, or running away from a bullet, we'll never know."

"Hey, look." Lauren plucked one of the girl's cell phone out of her hand and held it up. "It's still recording."

"Grab the rest of them. They might have something useful on them." I crouched down next to the girls, then shook my head sadly. "Typical really. Everybody's dying and they're uploading videos to social media. I wonder how many videos are in the cloud right now, each one catching the last moments of their lives because they didn't have enough sense to run and hide."

It was a sobering thought. Thanks to modern technology, this was going to be the most documented apocalypse in the history of mankind, all done close up and personal. The ultimate reality TV experience that would never make the ratings. There wasn't any viewing audience left to vote.

"We can check them later. I really think we should get out of here before whoever chained the doors and did this comes back," I said, gesturing to the universe at large. We had a bit of real estate to cover. The Zombie Mobile was parked in the back near the loading docks and so was Paul and Lauren's pickup truck, along with all the other vendors.

"I will be so glad to get to my arrows, an empty quiver is bullshit," KL mumbled.

I knew what she meant. My gun was in the truck too, and I knew that I would feel a lot better with it.

"Then again..." KL said before taking off at a jog, veering off to the left towards the next row of cars and leaving me to follow.

She had spotted the familiar light bar and cow catcher on an almost new Dodge Charger that marked it as a police vehicle.

"Please be open, please be open, please be open," KL muttered hopefully as we drew closer. Very carefully, she sidled up along the side of the vehicle and tried the door handle. It hadn't closed all the way and it swung open with a little help from her sword blade.

"Is it empty?"

"It's empty," she said, eagerly crawling inside the cab. "Fuck, it's not empty." She was back out on the pavement in a flash, chest heaving and a pissed off expression on her face. "Goddamn, mother-effing son of a bitch."

An impressive string of curse words followed, flowing from her lips without restraint. "Damn thing scared the hell out of me."

The cop was missing, but he had left someone behind. Cuffed in the backseat, we had a juicy little hoodlum zombie making quite the mess of himself. With nothing else to eat, he had turned on himself, creating a nightmare scene of gnawed bones and exposed tendons at each wrist in an animalistic attempt to free himself from the restraints.

"That would do it," I said, taking a quick peek inside. "Um, don't they usually cuff them behind their back?"

"Yes."

"Do I want to know how he got his cuffs in front of him?"

"Probably not."

"Okay. Let's move on," I said, watching the starved zombie attack the cage over and over again. I wasn't willing to turn my back on it until I was sure the mesh would hold.

"This is a waste of time," KL said after a quick search of the interior earned us nothing. "No shotgun, no shells, nothing."

"Mm. Not so fast," I said, holding up the keys I had found sitting in the ignition. "We have these."

"Trunk?" she asked, her eyes lighting up.

I chuckled. "Yep, let's see what's hiding behind door number two."

"Yeah, buddy."

It was Christmas in July, well, May right there in that trunk and KL was as happy as a kid in a candy store...if candy came in flat black and shiny brass and smelled like gunpowder and pain.

The trunk was full of flack gear and a couple of shotguns...a little overkill for a comic book convention if you asked me, but hey...I didn't create this screwed up world, I just live in it. Right now I was thanking all the crazy folk who weren't happy with the way the government was doing business, they were the reason Mr. Suburban Cop here had his trunk packed for the off chance there was an insurrection planned next week.

We took what we wanted and shut the trunk, then called Jason over.

"Hey Jason, you still driving that little subcompact around?" I asked, referring to what we affectionately called the clown car. What possessed the biggest men to find the smallest car to toodle around in was a mystery to me. Plastering something I could fit into my truck bed with Zombie Response Team stickers just made it more laughable.

"Yeah?"

I threw him the keys. "Why don't you upgrade today? It could come in handy just in case we have to drive faster than Fred Flintstone can peddle." The way I figured it, lights and sirens might give us a free pass depending on the situation.

Jason's jaw dropped and he stared at the sleek lines of the Charger with delight. "Really?"

"Really." I tossed him one of the shotguns and a box of shells. "Here. Just in case you have to make it look real."

We started walking away. KL grinned at me then turned around so she wouldn't have to yell and she could see his face. She always did enjoy delivering good news. "Yeah, but you might want to clear out the backseat first. It's going to need a thorough hosing when you get a chance. Your choice."

Jason peeked into the back seat and jumped back. "Shit, KL. That was fucked up."

She waved at him and Bobby and chuckled. "Yeah, yeah. We'll be around with the truck in a few minutes. Make sure you two are ready to roll by then."

Lauren, Paul and Ann rejoined us. Now that we were down two adults we could easily fit the rest of the crew in the back seat of the Zombie Mobile. Carol Ann could easily sit on Ann's lap. I sure as hell wasn't going to worry about child safety laws right now.

"That was pretty mean, what you did to Jason," Lauren scolded us, trying to sound all motherly and stern. Too bad she couldn't hide the smirk hiding behind that stern exterior because all it took was me cocking my head at her, all innocent like, to make her break down and giggle.

"Did you just giggle?" KL asked, acting horrified at the suggestion. "I don't think giggling is authorized during a zombie apocalypse."

"Screw you."

Ann's eyes widened, shocked at the wordplay. "You might as well get used to it, Ann. They always insult each other like this," I said. "They think it's fun."

"Oh. I'm coming with you?"

"Of course, both you and Carol Ann. You don't think we'd leave you behind?" It was sort of unfair to ask that, considering she'd already seen how mercenary we could be. The relief on her face was palpable. I thought I was going to have to fend off a pending hug so I stepped back, just in time to get clipped by something large and rock hard.

"What the fuck?"

"That's Brandon's Jeep."

"Babe? Are you okay?" KL's face floated above me. Everybody was yelling at the same time and I couldn't figure out why.

"I'm fine. Let me up," I huffed, pushing myself up off of the pavement. The concern in KL's eyes changed to pure fury once she was satisfied that all my parts still moved and I could talk in complete sentences.

"I'm going to kill that bastard," she hissed, casting about for her sword blade.

"You'll have to get behind me," Lauren spat. She was kneeling next to Paul, who was conscious and sitting up but obviously hurt. "I think his arm might be broken."

All we could do was watch Brandon leave us behind. I wasn't ready to use the shotguns until I knew it wouldn't bring every government entity in bright white hazmat suits down on us. KL growled in frustration and even ran a few steps after him, her hand reaching for non-existent arrows in her quiver.

"Goddammit, fucking asshole," she shouted, kicking an imaginary rock I knew she wished was the coward's head. "I'm sorry, Lauren. Paul."

If the douchebag had been paying attention, maybe he would have seen the Charger bearing down on him from the parking lot. Jason hit Brandon's Jeep just behind the front wheel well, pushing it off the pavement and onto the artificial hills built up around the convention center. The bright red Jeep bounced and almost tipped, then crashed into the chain link fence and stopped. A thin trail of smoke escaped from under the bent hood, but that was it. Brandon was either too injured to move or was dead, either one would work.

Serves him right, I thought. Someone behind me actually said it.

I noticed no one asked if we should go check on him. Maybe they were learning a few things from us. That couldn't be a bad thing, it might just get them through this alive.

"You guys ready already or what?" Jason called out to us.

"Stop being so damned impatient, dude. It's not like any of us have to get to work in the morning," KL yelled, then turned her attention back to Lauren and Paul.

"Let's get him into the truck. We'll figure out what to do once we're on the road."

"Aw, fuck." Lauren stopped dead in her tracks and whimpered. "Is this day never going to end?"

We all turned to see what had caught her attention. Damn, she was right. This day was never going to end.

KL

"Seriously?" First Brandon and now another group of zombies? "Does the man not know how to close a fucking door?"

A perfectly good, solid metal fire door had been rendered completely useless because Brandon left the damned thing open on the way out. Now we had a fresh wave of zombies wandering out onto the loading bay, and they weren't looking for a smoke break. We had about as much distance to go to get to our truck as they did, so it became a simple footrace to see who would get there first. It wasn't fair that they didn't have to use the stairs, not when they could just walk off the bay ledge and keep going. A few landed badly and had trouble getting back on their feet, so that helped. Watching them hobble forward on a broken leg that weebled when they wobbled did not.

I dug around in the gear bag and tossed Roxy one of the shotguns and a box of shells. We were too close now, the truck was right there and we were getting to it. Come hell or high water...or loud gun fire.

"Use it," I said to Roxy. We could deal with the government type people if they showed up later. Our boots hit against the unforgiving pavement with the same rumbling sound of a herd of horses, not a single one of us running in cadence with the other. Hell, I was thrilled to keep moving forward and not trip over my own feet. How Roxy did it while loading a shotgun at the same time? That was pure talent right there.

"Move over," she yelled, aiming the shotgun just to my left. It kicked hard against her shoulder and she winced in pain, but pumped it again and scanned for another victim. The report left my ears ringing and I remembered why I preferred archery to guns. They were too damned loud.

Roxy's sprinter didn't win a ribbon for first place, just a big ass hole in his head, but that didn't stop the rest of the crowd from trying to reach us.

"Too many," Roxy grumbled, picking her targets carefully before firing.

A loud screech as tires locked against the hot pavement made me jump. The Dodge Charger now stood between us and the remaining zombies, its powerful motor rumbled in the background, sounding quite pleased with itself. The cowcatcher on the front had taken a beating running into Brandon's Jeep but it was more than up to the task of turning the closest bunch of zombies into a flock of sailbunnies. Yes, Virginia, Superman can fly. He just doesn't land very well.

"Run, run for the fucking truck," Jason bellowed and pounded his palm against his door. I didn't need to be told twice. Carol Ann was slowing

Ann down too much, so I snatched her up and started booking for the rear passenger door. Of course it was locked and Roxy had the keys. The next few seconds felt scripted. A repeat of a hundred other times I stood at the door and waited for her to hit the button. Each time I would hold my temper and try not to get cranky while I got rained on or left out in the heat while she fiddle-fucked around with the button that electronically opened the door lock. Each time she would finally unlock the door and I would get in and give her a pissy look, then tell her that if she did that during a zombie apocalypse I would be zombie bait.

This time I was literally zombie bait while I waited for Roxy to hit the unlock button. "Come on, babe, just standing here during the zombie apocalypse," I yelled.

"Sorry, I was reloading," she apologized, then took down another zombie that was trying to skirt around the Charger's nose. It was a clean shot, but too low. The blast threw it backward a good three feet, left a Frisbee size hole in its chest and knocked a couple more zombies down in the process. Rather than get up and come after us, they stayed down, conveniently finishing the job for us. Why go after a meal that was still moving when something was right there, popped open like a can of spam.

Finally, after what felt like an eternity of heart stopping forced waiting, the truck beeped and I was able to open the back door. Ann popped in on the other side and held out her hands.

"Here, sweetie. Ann will watch you now. Hang tight, we'll be out of here in a pinch." She beamed up at me and nodded, sticking her little chin out bravely. In a rare moment of affection, I smiled back and gently chucked her under the chin. "Good girl."

Ann leaned over and pulled Carol Ann close, leaving as much room as possible for Paul and Lauren. They were close behind me the last time I checked, so when I heard a noise, I thought it was them. It wasn't.

"Sonofabitch," one word exhaled along with all the remaining air in my lungs before I hit the pavement. I had just enough time to bring my arm up in front of me before the damn thing latched on to me and knocked me off my feet. I tried to roll, but it was too heavy...heavy like the dead always were once they stopped breathing. Believe me, there's a noticeable difference. It's as if once the soul leaves, the meat that is left behind loses something intrinsic. Bread without the leavening, if you will.

Strange thoughts to be having while fighting for your very life. I balled up my fist and started pummeling it in the temple. My sword was somewhere close, but I couldn't reach it, and even if I could I didn't have any swinging room. This is why I always carry a knife...good for close up fighting and always enough room to wiggle between a rock and a hard-place, or in this case, my arm and a jawbone.

Not being able to take a decent breath was starting to hurt. I bunched up every muscle in my body and bucked as hard as I could, digging my heels into the pavement. "Get off me!"

"KL! Grab his head! Grab his hair and pull!" Lauren's voice came out of the fog that was quickly pulling me down into unconsciousness. I kicked out again and was able to catch a quick breath, enough to follow her directions.

Suddenly, the weight was gone but I was still holding onto a head by gleaming strands of blackish hair cut rakishly long along the brow. A bow tie fell on my chest and I swiped it off me with the same instinctual smack down I would have given a spider. Then I peeled the head away from my arm and held it up in front of me. The thing was surprisingly mobile for being detached from its body. I shuddered at the sensation, which was too close to how a tick felt squeezed between your fingers. You were never sure if the thing wouldn't pull an Atlas on you and push out of its prison before it got flushed.

"Oh man, and I really liked that version of The Doctor," I said, dismayed at finding out the zombie was dressed as one of my all-time favorite television characters.

"That's what you're going to worry about, right now? That thing bit you!" Lauren was, to put it simply, freaking out on me.

"No, it didn't." I held up my arm. My arm was firmly encased from fingers to elbow in my favorite leather bracer, it looked a little worse for wear after being a zombie chew toy, but it was definitely still intact. "I guess I have the Revenant Chaser to thank today, since this is her signature piece."

I turned to find Lauren standing over the back of the zombie with her knitting needles still in hand. The metal cord holding them together dripped wetly. The red drops hitting the pavement filled in the blanks that almost suffocating had left.

"Thanks, Lauren." It would have gotten me if she hadn't been there. "Let's get out of here."

I was almost afraid to utter those words, after the day we were having I was afraid I would jinx us yet again.

"Hey, is everyone okay?" Roxy showed up with Jason and Bobby in tow. I flashed Lauren a warning look that said do not tell her what happened. She didn't. She didn't know Roxy as well as I did, but believe me, neither of us wanted to deal with her when she was in overprotective mode.

"All good," I said, not offering any explanation for the decapitated zombie at our feet.

"Good. We finally got a break. The door wasn't jammed open so it finally closed on its own."

"It won't last." Yeah, that was me, the voice of doom.

All of us piled in, except for Lauren. After making sure Paul was comfortable with a makeshift sling wrapped around his injured arm, she bent down and picked up the decapitated head and climbed into the back of the truck with it.

Roxy started the truck and rolled the back window down. "What the hell, Lauren?"

"Just trust me. Go, go. More are coming from the front entrance." Standing in the truck bed gave her a better view than we had. If she said there were more coming it was time to leave.

Luckily Roxy had backed in this morning. Not in preparation for the world coming to an end but because she hates getting blocked in, and a big truck is easier to pull out of tight spaces. The Zombie Mobile was a big truck with big tires, so when she pulled out we ended up rolling over a really big bump. The suspension bounced and I felt my stomach twist and jump.

"Ugh, can we try not to do that again?" I would love to say we just sped off into the sunset, our little adventure over once we got into our truck, but that really wasn't possible. The parking lot was too crowded and not just with vehicles. There were bodies everywhere, and they weren't parked in neat little rows you could easily avoid. They might have been dead, but I had a hard time being so callous as

227

to just drive over them like so many speed bumps. It just didn't feel right.

"I'll do my best."

Jason pulled in right behind us and we started on our way.

Roxy slowed down as we passed Brandon's Jeep. He wasn't dead. The Jeep rocked back and forth, the engine racing dangerously close to redline with every attempt to free itself from the deep trench.

"How did I not hear that?" I asked, appalled at both my inattention and the fact that the douchebag was still moving.

Paul managed to laugh despite his pain. "We were all preoccupied with staying alive.

"Lauren noticed," Carol Ann piped up. I twisted around in my seat. She was just sitting there, her legs dangling off of a seat much too big for her and swinging her feet back and forth like little kids often did.

"What?"

"Lauren noticed. I think she's not very happy with him," Carol Ann said, then seemed to lose interest in the conversation. She tugged on Ann's shirt. "I'm thirsty."

"We'll find something to drink soon, okay?" She smoothed Carol Ann's hair and held her close, but her face told a different tale. She looked confused. Confused and a little bit disturbed.

Right there with you, sister.

"Do you think we should stop and help him?" Roxy asked, slowing the truck down to a crawl.

"Are you freaking kidding me?" I asked, almost giving myself whiplash when a high pitched scream practically crawled into the truck cab with us.

Lauren started laughing hysterically behind us. "Yes! Got you, you bastard."

Then she crawled back in through the back window and plopped herself down on the seat next to Paul. She was grinning from ear to ear, and was empty handed. I doubted she had left a zombie head bouncing around in the back of the truck, so that just left one other option. Judging from the way the Jeep was bouncing around and the shrill screams coming from its interior, I had a pretty good idea where that zombie head had gone.

"You didn't?" I asked, leaving it at that.

Lauren shrugged, her eyes flashing with barely contained disgust. "It's bad enough he left us and ruined our escape, he didn't have to try and mow us down with his car, too."

I had to agree with her. "I really like your style."

"Thank you."

For the first time since this morning, I felt like I could safely relax for a moment. We were armed, we had a small army that was coming together nicely as a team, and we were on our way home. I

229

kicked up my feet onto the dash, took off my hat, and sighed in relief. "Finally, we can go home now."

"We can't go home yet," Roxy mumbled. She kept her eyes on the road and refused to look over at me.

"Paul?" I knew his arm was in a bad way. I flipped down the visor and watched him from the vanity mirror. He looked very pale and sweaty.

"Yeah, he needs more help than we can give him with what we have."

"Shit." I sat back up in my chair. "This is going to suck. You know that, right? Fucking zombies at a hospital."

That's the last rule for now. It's never over. It will never be over. This is our new reality and nothing will ever be the same.

Sixty miles. Only sixty miles would get us home. Two hundred years ago that would have been farther than most people would ever travel in a lifetime. Yesterday it was a distance most people wouldn't have blinked an eye at. Today? We'll just have to see. The only guaranteed straight shot I trusted right now was an arrow or a bullet. Everything else was squirrely as hell.

4 p.m. (Same Day-The first day of the rest of the Apocalypse)

Well folks, that's how the apocalypse started for us. I hope since you are reading this that you have a safe place to ride this thing out.

My job is not to find out what caused it, but to survive.

I wish you all a safe apocalypse. We will try and update our adventures as we have time.

See ya' on the flip side.

Till then,

KL and Roxy.

KL's Rules for Zombie Hunting

Rule #1: Always go into an unknown situation with an empty bladder. You can run faster.

Rule #2: Know your limitations. If you weren't a world class athlete before the zombie apocalypse, don't assume you are one now.

Rule #3: Don't contemplate the how's or why's of the zombie apocalypse while fighting a zombie.

Rule #4: Don't lay down your weapon. Someone else might pick it up to use   against you.

Rule #5: Honor and fighting fair have no place in a zombie apocalypse.

Rule #6: Don't use movies as your base of knowledge.

Rule #7: Know how to use your weapon of choice. A zombie apocalypse is not the time to learn a new skill.

Rule #8: Don't keep the coward alive. They will just endanger you.

Rule #9: Keep a sense of humor. Nobody wants a downer to rain on the apocalypse.

Rule #10: Never assume a zombie is dead unless you did the killing.

Rule #11: The last and most important one: The apocalypse will never be over. This is the new reality, so don't think you can ever truly rest.

The History of the Revenant Chaser

It came about in a time of darkness and blood that one was born to do what no other could.

Revenants, the soulless remains of men and women alike, roamed the countryside. Lacking a soul, and not understanding their hunger, they preyed on the living...drinking their blood and on occasion, devouring their flesh.

No one knows where the Soulless come from, or why they hunt the night with screams that chilled even the hardest bones.

There are many stories, and none know how much truth they held, only that they existed and they made the world a more dangerous place.

Some say they are all that is left of a human after a vampire feeds from them too often and too deep, leaving nothing but a carcass in its wake that does not yet realize it should be dead.

Others say they are the failed remains of those who sought immortality voluntarily and failed to wake the next night, the poison blood of their potential maker animating their body but driving them insane.

Still other's claim they were not human at all, that they were the starved remnants of another race, an older race that was forced from their lands

235

and abandoned by their God's long before their people settled here and put the land to the plow. They argue that the revenants came when the first church was built, awakened by the stones being torn from the earth, angry that the Earth's bones were turned into strong walls to separate the faithful from the pagan lands around them.

Whatever the cause, the people lived in fear of these revenants. With the howls of demons announcing their arrival, they would arrive in the night...decimating entire towns with all the ravenous need of a pack of disease maddened wolves.

Within this world, The Revenant Chaser wandered. She had no name, at least not one she would volunteer to another soul. When asked, she would say she had given it away. Like the revenants she pursued, she had a sole purpose in life, teaching creatures that had forgotten what it was to fear to fear her.

She did not hunt. Hunting implied killing something that was still alive...and the revenants did not have enough life in them to warrant that consideration. She reminded them of their lost humanity, then gave them absolution by bringing them the only peace they will ever have, that of the grave.

The people never questioned why the Revenant Chaser did what she did, nor that she did so without any desire for recompense...they only felt relief at being saved by the mysterious woman in black.

Maybe they should have questioned. Maybe then they would not have called her hero and spoke of her with awe and reverence.

They would have seen her as what she was. A survivor.

If you enjoyed this novel, please check out more offerings by Rhavensfyre.

Follow on Facebook @ Characters of Rhavensfyre

www.rhavensfyre.com

twitter@rhavensfyre

46213528R00137

Made in the USA
Charleston, SC
13 September 2015